"DEAD LOW"

For Rich & Chloe *Corbett Davis*

"DEAD LOW"

Corbett A. Davis Jr.

Library of Congress Control Number:		2013914474
ISBN:	Hardcover	978-1-4836-8351-5
	Softcover	978-1-4836-8350-8
	Ebook	978-1-4836-8352-2

Rev. date: 08/09/2013

To order additional copies of this book, contact:
Xlibris LLC
1-888-795-4274
www.Xlibris.com
Orders@Xlibris.com
134073

For Corbett Davis IV and Mia Kathryn Davis,
two beacons of joy that light up my ocean.

"The sea, once it casts its spell, holds one in its net of wonder forever."

—Jacques Yves Cousteau

"We must free ourselves of the hope that the sea will ever rest. We must learn to sail in high winds."

—Aristotle Onassis

"The boisterous sea of liberty is never without a wave."

—Thomas Jefferson

Acknowledgments

When Powell Taylor looks back at his childhood, as he often does these days, there was nothing misspent about his youth.

Growing up on Pensacola Bay provided the perfect setting that taught him great appreciation for life, the environment, and the importance of family and friends. In his adolescent years, Powell allowed himself no idle times, no squandered moments. Throwing his cast net; chasing mullet, crab boils, and fish fries; and traveling in his skiff with a ten-horse Johnson were as much a part of his life as math class, football games, and sock hops were for others. The bay was home. Over the early years, it would teach him conservation, awareness, and a respectful fondness for the environment.

Many times, Powell's family would stand barefoot in ankle-deep water in a circle heel to toe with each other. His dad, Charles Sr., would find the biggest blue crab in the trap and drop him in the middle of their circle of toes. He would warn them, "Don't move or he'll bite you." They all would laugh and shake as the hungry crab walked over their feet watching for the slightest movement so he could grab a toe and pinch it like a pecan in a nutcracker. Powell's brother, Bradford, almost always had black-and-blue reminders of his inability to keep still.

By the time the sun disappeared behind the Pensacola skyline, they had not only boiled up that crab and all his buddies but had also spent the day enjoying family and friends. Pensacola Bay brought them all together.

The author, Powell, and Limbo would like to thank some of those friends for their help and inspiration with *Dead Low*.

Thanks to Jimbo Meador, a dear friend whose love of fly-fishing and vast knowledge on the environment were invaluable to Powell and Limbo throughout their adventure.

Thanks to all of my fishing friends that have allowed me to share the bow of a boat or a secluded flat with them. You all know who you are. It is these experiences that jump-start my imagination.

Others who deserve thanks and appreciation for their help and technical knowledge include Bobby Likis, Dr. Norman McFadden Jr., the crew of the Square Grouper Restaurant on Cudjoe Key, Connie and the staff at JTS Jewelry Store in Pensacola, and Carlos and Flora who were always kind to Powell Taylor.

I would like to send a much-deserved thank-you to John D. McDonald, Randy Wayne White, and Carl Hiaasen. Their notable characters including Travis McGee, Doc Ford, and Skink inspired Powell and Limbo on their trek through Florida.

Special thanks to my dad who injected the saltwater of Pensacola Bay into my veins at a very early age.

And lastly, thanks to my wife, Theresa, who not only edited my pages but also helps me dot my i's and cross my t's daily.

Corbett A. Davis Jr.

CHAPTER 1

I glared into a stained and broken mirrored glass hanging in the dim-lit back room of Coco's Cantina. As I hugged the top of a porcelain urinal, I did not like the reflection that peered back from one half-closed, bloodshot eye. It was not just the weathered face, the long hair, the dark circles under lifeless eyes, or the beer-stained shirt that hung from my shoulders that bothered me so. It was more, much more. Through those dead eyes, I looked deep into a black soul, a soul that had transformed over the last year and a half. If I had any idea of the hell the next months would bring, I simply would not give a damn now. My life was about to turn into a horror movie. What had happened to me? How could I have let this occur?

Although my mind was completely garbled at this moment, I knew exactly what had happened. Three years ago, with some good luck, hard work, and certain unusual circumstances, I had it all. My friends and family call me Powell, but my full name proudly appeared on many certificates, documents, and licenses. "Charles Powell Taylor Jr." is how it read on my diploma from Florida State University, my boat captain's license, my private pilot's license, and my gemologist degree from the Gemological Institute of America. These were my most meaningful accomplishments to date. I was hoping to add one more notable document real soon, a marriage license. By the early age of thirty, I had the world figured out. Thanks to an upbringing in a family retail jewelry business, I knew love, responsibility, and discipline. Along with that good luck I spoke about, I owned and ran the most successful jewelry store in the Keys.

Caribbean Jewelry Company is located on Duval Street in downtown Key West, Florida. Key West is an unusual city and destination for hundreds of thousands of tourists each year. Cruise ships line up daily on the docks off Mallory Square and dump out plenty of sunburned tourists with fat wallets. The airport is small but is very busy transporting fishermen, divers, businessmen, gays, lesbians, vacationers, honeymooners, writers, musicians, actors, ladies, gentlemen, rednecks, hillbillies, and pirates to America's southernmost city. The chain of forty-two bridges connecting all the islands into Key West brings the remainder of tourists to this colorful city located just ninety-one miles north of Cuba.

Besides fine jewelry and a laid-back attitude, Key West is known for many great things. Cause for the gravitational pull south includes breathtaking sunsets, reef diving, fishing, sunken treasures, architecture, art, famous ghosts, bikinis, and plenty of cold fruity rum drinks.

But not everyone is able to keep the pace for very long. Many of those tourists in bermuda shorts and flip-flops—the Ernest Hemingway, Jimmy Buffett, and Mel Fisher wannabes—run out of energy, money, or both. Too much sun, booze, and drugs. Too much time wasted. Not enough responsibility, no time to think, and far too many dead brain cells.

And all of that brings us back to me at this moment in my life. I am living proof of "the Keys disease." I am wasting away in Jimmy B's "Margaritaville" like so many others before me.

My business has been affected, many of my friendships have been lost, my love life with Dawn is questionable, I am thirty pounds overweight, and I have pissed away all my cash. And that would be a bunch of cash!

If someone would shove a parrot up my ass and get a photo of me wearing my Hawaiian shirt, Corona with a slice of key lime in hand posed in front of that butt-ugly red, white, and black southernmost buoy, I would make a great front cover for a new Buffett album, *Dumb Ass in Paradise*. I was not proud of what I saw in the mirror. I was ashamed.

It seemed like only yesterday I was in perfect shape, happy, and in love with the girl of my dreams. I was thin, pretty, and rich, living on things that intrigued me. I always thought of myself as living life at high tide, where everything is clear and beautiful. The push of high water flushes out the old and dingy stench of rotting seaweed that clouds the bays throughout the Florida straits. I enjoy living in that environment, one of precise clarity. I stayed in shape by swimming three miles a day, eating healthy, and only drinking a beer or two occasionally. But look at me now. I am out of shape, am drunk, and look like shit. What the hell happened to me over the last eighteen months? It was a rhetorical question because I knew exactly what caused this change. The tide had fallen quickly in my life. I was now living life at the lowest of tides, clouding my thoughts, my lifestyle, and my unstable, blemished, and tarnished inner core.

I gazed out the dingy amber-stained bathroom window. Coco's parking lot was filled with an assortment of vehicles. There were cars, trucks, Harleys, and even a tour bus filling every available space in the oyster-shell lot. I could now clearly hear the music that was playing on the jukebox out front. A few locals sang along with Alan Jackson. Most of them probably thought they sounded like the country star. Even in my condition at the moment, I knew that none of them would be recording music anytime soon. It was a sad sound. Then I heard everyone in the restaurant sing aloud, "It's five o'clock somewhere," followed by some loud hooting and hollering. Then everything went mute as something caught my eye and made the hair on the back of my neck stand up like porcupine quills. A nervous blob of tension bottomed out in the pit of my stomach. A little two-door white Mercedes coupé pulled into the parking lot looking for an empty space. It was a car exactly like the one I had bought for Dawn on her twenty-seventh birthday last year. It was a sight that almost sobered me up. The anticipation of seeing Dawn step out of that car brought a sudden smile to my face. The smile hurt. My head and wrinkled forehead were throbbing to an echo of my heartbeat. Even my hair hurt. I had not seen or heard from Dawn in more than two weeks. Dawn was the only girl I have every really loved. But she was pissed off now, and so was I. She had every reason to be. I did not. I had tried to call and apologize, but she was never home. At least she never answered the phone. Maybe she would listen to me now.

My heart missed a beat when the door of the Benz opened and a cute little coffee-skinned Cuban girl stepped out. It was not Dawn at all.

I pulled out a letter from my shirt pocket and tried to focus. The letter was dated August fourteenth, two days ago, and was mailed from the post office on Summerland Key. She started by saying how upset she was and what an asshole I was. Four pages later, Dawn closed with "I'll love you forever." It was a disturbing letter for sure, but she was now ready to talk to me. That was a good sign.

I opened the door of the restroom and stepped into the main part of the restaurant. Carlos was at the stove cooking when he looked up and waved to me asking, "You okay, amigo?" I assured him all was good. Carlos had been a good friend since I arrived here in the Keys five years ago. He and his wife Flora ran the restaurant and always looked out for me when I needed a friend.

I went outside and pushed the speed dial on my cell phone for Dawn's phone number. Just like the last thousand or so times, the familiar voice of her recording greeted me. Something did not feel right about this. In her letter, she said she needed to talk to me as soon as possible. That was two days ago. Sensing that something bad was wrong here, I decided to

Corbett A. Davis Jr.

drive to Key West, find her, and talk with her. I will tell her how sorry I am and what she means to me. I will make everything just like it was before. She was right. I had been an asshole.

Being way too drunk to drive to Key West, it would have to wait until "manana." I asked Carlos if he could give me a ride home. He was too busy in the kitchen but said his daughter would be happy to take me. Carlos and Flora were two of the very few friends I had left. Their daughter Lily was eighteen years old, tall, thin, and beautiful with skin the color of a perfect cinnamon tan. She and Flora looked more like sisters than mother and daughter.

When I arrived home, I sat down at my desk, still drunk, and scribbled out a list of things I wanted to change in my life. In the morning, I hoped that I would take it seriously and not change my mind.

CHAPTER 2

Dawn Landry is a beautiful twenty-eight years of age. In the past five years since she moved to the Florida Keys, Dawn has spent much of her time getting into shape. Every morning, she awakes at five o'clock with no alarm clock or wake-up call. She is a perfectly focused, disciplined creature of habit. By five fifteen, she had changed into her swimsuit and taken her daily seven-mile swim. From the house on Cudjoe Key, she swims a series of connecting canals out into Cudjoe Bay. She returns home following her same track an hour and a half later. She had lost twenty-five pounds over the last couple of years by working out religiously and eating healthy. She was the most physically fit she had ever been.

Unfortunately, Dawn's nightmare started a few weeks ago. She and Powell had once been so much in love. They seemed to enjoy each other every moment of every day. They laughed, kidded around, complimented each other, held hands, and had pillow fights. They sipped wine, listened to music, and took boat rides together. They worked out, cooked out, watched rental movies, ate junk food, talked, and deeply understood each other. They also had the most amazing sex together, more so than either of them had ever experienced. Dawn felt she had met her one and true soul mate for life. Powell knew he had found the lady of his dreams. It had been six years since they met in Boca Grande. Dawn was a teller in a local bank. It was love at first sight when Powell came in to cash a check and ask for directions. Six months later, Dawn moved to the Keys to be with the man she loved. Powell bought a house on Cudjoe Key, just twenty-two miles east of Key West with plans of living happily ever after. Most of the years spent there were magical for them both. They enjoyed their time together. They wanted to be together at all times, but as is often the case, something had changed recently. Their feelings were different. Love faded into doubt as fun and happiness turned into boredom. They spent more time distancing themselves and talking less. Dawn and Powell faced the fact that they were falling out of love. Powell started drinking heavily to forget while Dawn tried to forget Powell. The money became tight, the arguments started to heat up, and they both developed other interests. Dawn worked out, swam, ran, and concentrated on health and herself even more than before. Powell turned to liquor, ate excessively, and fished too much. Hanging out in marinas took its toll on him. The unhappiness made him a different person. He hated himself, and Dawn was beginning to feel the same way. It had been three weeks since Dawn moved out and rented a little loft over Hurricane Hole Marina in Key West. They thought that if they separated they would have time to think about it all and then maybe things would work out.

It did not take long for Powell to realize that you don't know what you have until it's gone. He was feeling depressed and lonely. Powell missed Dawn and wanted her back. He wanted their lives together, but feared it may be too late. The thought of losing her forever made him sick to his stomach. The arguing, the separation, and the stress had taken its toll on Dawn also. She had become fanatical about exercising and losing weight. She was borderline anorexic and knew it. After swimming, running, and playing tennis on one afternoon, she was at home doing her third set of one hundred crunches. She jumped up too quickly, and the room began to spin. As she passed out, she caught the edge of her bed with her head. She woke up in a pool of blood with a throbbing headache. Dawn called

Powell, got his answering machine, and left a message later realizing it sounded a little desperate. She then drove herself to the emergency room at Seaman's Hospital in Key West. Powell was at Coco's Cantina getting drunker by the minute.

When Dawn walked through the door of the hospital, the staff frantically ran to her side. She had not realized how bad she looked. Her body was a little too thin and her pretty blond hair stuck like tape to a glossy maroon blob matted to the side of her head. She was dizzy again. Dawn needed care, care that would include many tests, IVs, rest, and much time in the hospital.

Once she was in her room, she pulled out her phone and hit speed dial.

"Powell? Hey, it's me. Give me a call on my cell as soon as you get this message. I need to talk to you. I love you so much Powell."

When she hung up, the tears that filled her eyes blurred her vision.

Corbett A. Davis Jr.

CHAPTER 3

Anchored in the harbor at the far west end of the island was a unique looking ship. Not quite as large as the cruise ships docked beside her, she was still easily visible from Duval Street. As hundreds of tourists passed by each day, many comments could be heard aloud. It looks like a ghost ship," a woman in her early thirties commented. "Why don't they paint that rust bucket?" snapped a business executive from Atlanta. "What an eyesore. It's blocking such a beautiful view of the ocean," another bikini-clad tourist exclaimed.

The "ghost ship" frightened all of the children, attracted many curious visitors, and prompted remarks from almost everyone who saw her. Every person that passed by was captivated by the unusual aura that seemed to surround her hull like a demonic halo. The huge red cross painted beneath the bow on the port and starboard sides did not ease the visual pain. The ship still looked haunted.

It was a beautiful day in Key West. The sun was high and hot, the winds were calm, and you could see for miles across the deep blue passage of salt where the Gulf meets the Atlantic. Nevertheless, around the rusty old ship, a breathless haze hung closely like a fog hiding her mortal soul. For now, this black soul would be the only common ground that "the ghost ship" and Powell Taylor would share. However, things change quickly, and for Powell Taylor, their lethal union would come too soon. In the weeks to come, Powell would learn to respect her, fear her, and curse her very existence.

The *Lady Demonio*, as locals named her, was actually a 265-foot passenger vessel from Saudi Arabia. Her real name, although no longer legible on her stern, was *Star of Ashrafi*. She was originally built in 1957 in Pascagoula, Mississippi. In her day, the *Lady Demonio* was a beautiful ship that transported many passengers. Not the *Demon Lady* as she was now referred to by the Cuban population of Key West.

In 1957, R. I. Ingalls was proud to launch the SS *Brasil*, a super luxury liner, into the Pascagoula River. The 186th ship to be launched by Ingalls shipyard, the SS *Brasil*, cost twenty-five million dollars to build and was capable of speeds up to twenty-two knots. She had the most modern technical developments of any ship afloat. On a brisk December day in 1957, as the *Brasil* slipped down the tracks into the river, Mississippi was proud. An hour-long christening attended by many dignitaries turned into an all-day event. Along with fireworks, the music of the University of Southern Mississippi's band filled the air while locals prepared a celebratory Cajun crawfish boil. All this was happening while the poetic invocation was proudly being delivered by the bishop of the Natchez-Jackson Diocese. Hopefully, the bishop and the fine people of Mississippi would never learn the future state of the SS *Brasil*. In 1990, when the vessel seemed out of date and past its prime, a Saudi Arabian oil magnate purchased the SS *Brasil* for 27.5 million dollars. After two years of repairs and modernization, he renamed it *Star of Ashrafi*. Now almost fifty years later, the once-luxurious passenger ship is associated with demons and evil spirits.

One particularly ironic thing about the haunting boat is where the Saudi businessman had the newest upgrades completed. In 1990, he had the ship delivered to an eight-hundred acre shipyard, employing more than ten thousand employees on the Mississippi Coast. Thirty miles east of Gulfport in Pascagoula, the Ingalls shipbuilding yard would turn the

1957 passenger vessel into a floating state of the art hospital. The Saudi had supposedly found religion. Allah told him to do good in this life and use his wealth to help the world. The journey of the *Star of Ashrafi* would be long and tumultuous to say the least. It would be an unbelievable trek through hell. And she would drag a young, confused, lovesick jeweler along with her. Powell Taylor would never be the same after their courses collide.

CHAPTER 4

When the sun finally woke me at nine o'clock, my head was pounding, my temples were throbbing, and my mouth tasted as if I had eaten a roll of wet toilet paper. I pulled myself out of bed and stumbled to the kitchen to make some strong café con leche using my favorite dark-roasted Cuban beans. Taped to the coffee maker was the envelope from my telephone bill with my pathetic list of resolutions. I tried to focus and read what I had scratched out in red ink. I had a difficult time trying to translate.

1. Do'Not be ashole
2. Quite drinking two much
3. Xcersize and get shape
4. Aopyig appollojiz tell Dawn I'm Sorry!
5. Look up ole friends and call em and talk long tim
5. Tell Dawn how much I love her
7. Call Mom, Daddy and
8. Call Bradford toooo
9. Go fishin with Limbo
12. Be nice all times
13. Work more/have meeting with employ—
14. Save monie
15. Make Lily a peace of jewelry
16. Go to confessin/make Mama happy

I didn't know whether to laugh or cry.

It was a sad moment as I read and reread the list. My first inclination was to rip up the envelope and burn it, never to be seen again. But after much thought, I decided it looked better pinned to the front of my fridge with a little bonefish magnet. Every day it would remind me of the depth I allowed myself to descend to. It was time for recovery.

I glanced outside responding to a subtle movement that called my eye. A small flock of white ibis was foraging my lawn while probing for insects below the turf. Their long decurved bills swept back and forth like a spoonbill. A young immature ibis with mostly brown coloring was learning to search for his own food while slowly walking. Soon he will be able to follow his parents to the marshes and probe for fiddler crabs in holes, as well as chasing crabs on the surface. The young ibis will learn to alternate between probing and visual foraging. Watching this happy family of birds reminded me that ibises are monogamous and care by both parents is necessary for successful rearing of their young. I looked back at my list and focused on number 4.

Dawn and I had discussed marriage and kids on a few occasions. Once again, I dialed her phone number. The same message began that I've heard for the last two weeks. As I was leaving her an apology and telling her how much I loved her, a bewildering thought hit me like a ton of bricks. It had been days since I checked messages on my own cell phone. My mind and my body both had been too drunk to focus and function. What a dumb ass! Here I was leaving message after message assuming she did not want to talk to me. Now I found that I had thirteen messages in the past four days, all from Dawn. Her tone started as a pissed off attitude. She was obviously mad at me. In later messages, she forgave me. Then she even missed me, loved me, and needed me with her for eternity. I was grinning, jumping up and down, until I heard the last message. Yesterday, at five in the afternoon, Dawn frantically told me she had fainted and hit her head. She seemed quite delirious. The blood drained from my head, and the smile departed my face leaving an aching pain. I grabbed my keys and ran toward the Tahoe while pressing the door release. I jumped in, sped out of Cudjoe Gardens, and headed west toward Key West on U.S. 1. Seaman's Hospital was twenty-two miles away. Seventeen minutes later, I was running through the front door. The news I got was not good. Dr. M. Shezad, a young intern walking past the desk on the third floor, finally decided to talk to me. Dawn was exhausted and anemic, with strong symptoms of anorexia. The doctor assured me she would be fine. They had her in intensive care overnight with IVs renourishing her frail body. I could see her Thursday morning after she was in a private room.

"What is today?" I thought. It was only Tuesday. These upcoming thirty-six hours not only would prove to intensify my agony and guilt but also would haunt my nights and turn dreams into nightmares for a very long time.

If only I could talk with her, hold her, and see that she is okay or hear her voice breathe softly in my ear.

With no emotion, the doctor turned away as he grunted, "You can see her Thursday and not before."

Corbett A. Davis Jr.

CHAPTER 5

No one could ever mistake me for being anorexic I thought as I made a U-turn into the Waffle House parking lot. I felt like Dawn was safe for now. She was in good hands, and I would finally be able to see her soon. Butterflies in my stomach reminded me how much I missed being with her. We became so routine that we took each other's company for granted. I swore that would never happen again.

"Good evening. Welcome to Waffle House," a tired looking but attractive young girl said as I entered the door. Her nametag read Tracy. It only took a couple of unexpected minutes to learn way too much about the cute and overly friendly waitress. She was from Mobile, Alabama and had lived in Key West for three years. She wasn't married, had a five-year-old daughter, and was going to the junior college when she wasn't working. I introduced myself and gave her the short version of my life also. For some reason, I did not mention Dawn to Tracy.

Tracy handed me a menu with big color pictures. Many nights after drinking too much, I had pointed at this menu to order. I pointed again at a big bowl of grits, a waffle, and a cup of coffee.

"Wow. This menu has words too." I thought. Reading about the Waffle House was pretty amazing. The next newsletter from Caribbean Jewelers could use some of this style with excitement and interesting facts.

"Damn!" I thought as I read aloud, "408,165,000 waffles sold since 1955." The menu was reading as if I had googled Waffle House trivia. Why had I never noticed this before? It was an encyclopedia of facts written in small print visible only to the sober, hungry crowds that did not just point to colorful pictures. How in the hell can you prepare a hamburger over twenty-two million ways?

By the time I finished my waffle and bowl of grits, I had learned much more about Waffle House than I wanted to know. The world's leading server of cheese and eggs, raisin toast, grits, omelets, and apple butter also serves hash browns seven different ways. I grimaced instantly as I realized my life at this moment was like Waffle House hash browns. It was scattered, smothered, and covered.

"Are you okay?" Tracy asked when she brought the bill. "Yeah, I'm fine, just somewhere else right now," I replied.

Tracy then surprised me and said, "I get off in an hour, and I hear the tarpon are running off Woman Key."

"You fish?" I asked.

"Of course, but only with a fly rod," she exclaimed. A girl after my own heart, I thought. Tracy was a beautiful girl with a sensual southern dialect. She was maybe twenty-five or twenty-six years old, thin, had brown hair, and big blue eyes. Her smile was inviting and sensuous. Tracy had deeply tanned skin, thin facial features, and thick lips. In a different time, I would have been eager to tarpon fish with Tracy. But tonight I had only one thing on my mind, Dawn. Dawn Landry, the love of my life.

"Sorry Tracy, I can't but maybe some other time," I said.

"Well, if you change your mind Powell Taylor, give me a call. There are two Tracys here so make sure you ask for Tracy Lewis."

We chatted awhile, and I told her if she got downtown to come by and see me at the jewelry store. She said she would definitely see me again. I felt a little guilty knowing how much I was attracted to her. She was not only beautiful, sexy, and interesting, but she also liked to fly-fish.

Corbett A. Davis Jr.

Thursday morning could not come soon enough. I would be back at the hospital bright and early with much to say to Dawn. I would confess my sins to her. My Catholic upbringing always put a guilt trip on me. Confession is good for the soul. Twelve years of Catholic education taught me this. I would acknowledge my sins to Dawn. I'm sorry for past behavior and for not showing how much I love you.

I am sorry for the drinking, for the out of control lifestyle, and not paying attention to you.

I looked forward to salvaging my life, my love, and my business. The only thing I would not confess to would be my thoughts about Tracy. Tracy, the cute girl from Mobile, Alabama who loves to fly-fish. Father Johnny Licari from back home in Gulf Breeze would not agree. "Confess all," he would say.

CHAPTER 6

I couldn't sleep. The anticipation of finally seeing Dawn kept me awake all night. I was relieved she was okay, and yet I was nervous. I felt like a high school kid going on his first date. What would I say? How would I explain my stupidity over the past month? Would she believe me that I'm ready to repent? Should I beg for forgiveness? Mea culpa, mea culpa, mea maxima culpa, my most grievous fault!

A little after midnight, I put on an old Buffett album, poured myself some tawny port, grabbed a Montecristo from the humidor, and went outside. The awesome view from my wooden deck was welcome. Before I sat down, I called my buddy Limbo and told him I could use a friend. He didn't ask questions, just said, "I'll see you in about ten minutes."

The moon over Cudjoe Bay was bright, probably only a day or two before full. Although the sky was clear, there was uneasy energy in the air. With no wind or clouds, I could see flashing light on the western horizon, followed by a thunderous noise.

The eerie feeling eased considerably as I finished the first glass of port. I eyed the bottle of Taylor twenty-year Tawny as Buffett sang an old ballad of Spider John. If Dawn were here, life would be perfect. But of course, she wasn't. Between the Cuban tobacco, the Tawny, and the mesmerizing lyrics of early Buffett tunes, I slipped off into an abysmal sleep.

At first light, I was suddenly awakened by Limbo's voice.

"Is that the thanks I get? I get here at one o'clock in the fucking morning, and you're sound asleep, shitty music blaring, and you're about to set yourself on fire with a half-smoked stogie?"

Remotely disoriented, I try to focus in Limbo's direction. Captain Limbo stood there in the doorway dressed only in his underwear holding a large coffee cup. At the instant I recognized his giant grin, the aroma of fresh ground coffee beans also hit my senses. Café con leche! And Limbo would tell you it's the only vice he has left these days. At six foot two inches with broad shoulders and a thin waist, Captain Limbo has plenty of connections, a devious past, and is a great friend that has helped me out of some very bad situations in the last few years. His unclear past, even to me, has made him a careful, sober, and logical thinker. It also has made him paranoid, so paranoid it would lose him friends and family. So paranoid it would save his life and that of a young love-struck jeweler who dragged him into a deadly adventure.

When I first met Captain Limbo, I believed that he was old, tired, and a rude curmudgeon of a fishing guide. It was one of the few first impressions that I ever wrongly made. My first take on Limbo was derived by shallow means and physical appearance only. His dark weathered leather-like skin, his slow Southern drawl, his obvious scars from skin cancer cut off his face, and his casual attire of shorts, flip-flops, and very long billed cap were the reasons for my inaccurate conclusion. It was part of a character flaw I was working to eliminate. I would often judge people though usually accurately. And I had a problem forgiving and forgetting. Actually, I don't have a problem with forgiving, but I never forget.

Although a great fisherman, Captain Limbo was not a guide at all. He in fact was James Adams, had a doctorate in marine biology, and wrote many books in his field. Dr. Adams traveled the world, spoke at conventions, and taught at some of the best universities. Spending much of his time on the water, he became an expert on the impact that overfishing and excessive netting had caused on the marine environment. Captain Limbo was solely instrumental in starting a net ban in Florida waters.

He was responsible for the sudden and necessary boom in aquaculture. "Farming Shrimp for the Future" was not only Limbo's idea, it was also his passion and the name of the book that caught the eye of a large restaurant chain owner. Limbo now had a free pass to any and all Red Lobster restaurants worldwide. But that all happened a long time ago.

Between all that time on the water, all those Vietnam memories, all the money he made, and too much time in airports, Dr. James Adams was burned out. His training in Vietnam combined with all the hours spent on the water resulted in a relationship that now allowed Captain Limbo to work closely with U.S. Customs. As I found out a couple years ago, he only works occasionally and only on cases not publicized. His name or any connections with U.S. Customs will never surface. Not even if he was killed. And I knew in his line of work that was always a good possibility.

Limbo handed me a cup of coffee and said, "So what's up? Where the hell ya' been lately?"

We stepped out on the back deck to finish our coffee. A school of parrotfish was working the coral rock beneath the dock. Focused, very focused, their tails would drift toward the surface as they nibbled away on one particular section of coral. They were acrobatic and yet simultaneously quite clumsy.

"You didn't call me over here to watch your fuckin' fish, did you?" Limbo said with his shit eatin' grin. One thing about Limbo, he could always fit the F-bomb between syllables. "No, I didn't ask you over here to watch the fucking parrotfish," I replied. He grinned again.

I explained what was happening in my life, why he hadn't heard from me, and why we haven't fished together in almost a year now. Limbo's expression was one of concern and compassion. He could obviously feel my pain. I sensed he had been here before himself. And he would never say it, but I knew he noticed my bloodshot eyes, dark circles, and extra pounds. I assured him I was on the road to recovery and that as soon as Dawn was home we would have him back over for dinner.

He picked up the *Key West Times* and began to read the headlines. I didn't hear a word he said. I gotta call Dawn, it's almost eight o'clock. They had said I could talk with her today but could not see her till tomorrow."

Limbo nodded toward my phone in the other room never looking up from the paper.

"Hi, this is Powell Taylor. Could you connect me with Dawn Landry's room please? I think it's room 360," I said to the receptionist. "It's near intensive care." Without a word, the hold button was pushed, and I was listening to a prerecorded tape on why Seaman's Hospital is one of the ten best places in the United States to work. My heart was pounding with expectation. I had so much to say, so much to explain. I would never lose her again. My mind shifted back to the recording. We are proud to be in the top ten places . . . ."

I'm starting to get pissed now. Why so long of a wait? Why is this hospital advertising that it's a great place to work? Why don't they say Seaman's Hospital is in the top ten best places to be hospitalized or saved or cured or treated? Hell, I know a guy who works at a funeral home who loves his job and what he does. But I don't know anyone who wants to check in there.

Then I felt my grin, thinking of what Captain Limbo would be saying. "What the fuck is your problem? Answer the fucking telephone!"

"Hello."

I could hardly breathe when she finally answered.

"Hey, sweetheart, I miss you very much!" I blurted out so fast all the words ran together.

"I'm sorry, Mr. Powell, but Ms. Landry is still in intensive care."

"Taylor," I said, "my name is Powell Taylor." That's the problem with having two last names, I get called everything, Powell Taylor, Taylor Powell, Mr. Powell. Whatever. Why am I explaining this, and why do I care right now?

"She'll be in a private room late tonight, and you can see her at eight o'clock bright and early tomorrow morning, Mr. *Taylor*," she said with a nasty emphasis on *Taylor*.

"Thank you, Miss _____," I said, waiting for her to fill in her name.

"Eaton, Eve Eaton," she declared.

"Well, Ms. Eaton, is it true? Is Seaman's Hospital a great place to work?"

"Hardly," she yelled as she slammed down the phone.

I walked back out on the deck. The parrotfish had moved on to another section of coral bed. Limbo was still mesmerized with the newspaper.

"Man, this is just fucking gruesome, Powell," Limbo said as he pointed to a photo of an island that looked familiar.

"Is that Sawyer Key, Limbo?" I asked.

"Yeah, and they found two bodies floating out there yesterday. A male and a female that they think were in their late twenties."

"Think?" I said.

"Yep, the bodies were so ripped up; they aren't sure yet. They assume it was sharks, but I don't think so," he stated as Dr. James Adams. It was not Captain Limbo speaking. "Both bodies were missing their hearts and kidneys, and neither had eyes left in the sockets. Yet they still must have been intact enough to be able to identify their gender. That seems like quite a coincidence to me. Both bodies had the same injuries," he continued.

"Hey, Limbo, I remember a couple years ago some bodies were found at the back end of No Name Key with their hearts missing. I think it was some cult or some demon worshipers that were blamed. Did they ever catch those people?" I asked.

"I don't know, but this is too fucking weird if you ask me." He was Limbo again.

Since I couldn't talk to Dawn or see her until tomorrow morning, I decided to ask Limbo to join me for some afternoon fishing. It had been too long since we shared the bow of a boat together. Besides, it would be good to get my mind off Dawn, and the guilt I felt.

He quickly agreed. "Let's go."

CHAPTER 7

Dawn woke up in a cold sweat. At this very moment, she is not feeling well. Something in Dawn Landry's brain is wrong. Her thoughts are confused, distorted, as she drifts in and out of reality. She is in a bright place, a very bright, sanitary place. As her mind scrolls back to try and remember, she suddenly smiles. She hears laughter, her own laughter. But it is a muted sound, coming from within, vibrating from her vocal cords. It's as if she is seeing herself on TV, viewing her actions from inside herself as an observer across the room from her own limp body. Her head is full of live wires with no connection, making no sense whatsoever. A shadow crosses her lifeless face. Powell, is that you sweetheart?" She whispers with strong hopes. It was not Powell at all.

Abruptly, the electricity in her mind stops as she realized she is smiling aloud. She remembers how awkward it was to learn how to swim all over again just seven years ago. When Dawn turned twenty-one, she felt like she needed something to build her self-esteem. Not only did she increase her self-esteem, she increased her bust line to a 34DD. Of course it was unnecessary. Dawn was a gorgeous girl with a slight build, long thin legs, a flat belly, natural bronze skin, big blue eyes, and beautiful blond hair. But she always thought her breasts were too small. Her friends tried to tell her that she was well proportioned, and 34C was quite stunning on her. She didn't listen.

Now as Dawn lay on a cold stark table, she wondered why she was reminded of this. The smell of antiseptics was familiar. It was the same scent as seven years ago when Dr. Jacobs inserted her saline implants. She tried to focus on the foot of her bed, tried to see her toes and beyond. Who was there? All she could see were tits, beautiful firm 34DD tits. She smiled at her thoughts and then began to cry. The electricity came back like a wet finger in an electric socket. The spitting and sputtering of a live wire crossed between her petite ears. She felt fear, tried to pray. "Hail Mary full of grace. The Lord is with thee . . ." But it was no use, she was losing control. She was going down quick.

"Powell, I'm so sorry. I love you with all my heart" were the last words she muttered before total darkness fell over her. The electrical storm in her brain had ceased.

CHAPTER 8

My house is built on a wide canal at the water's edge of Cudjoe Bay. The colorful vegetation of plants and palm trees completely conceals the home from the road and from my neighbors. An old conch-style house built up on concrete blocks with stucco sides, it has a balcony on the upper level overlooking front and back. The front steps lead you into the main room overlooking the bay. It is a spacious, comfortable area with wooden floors, bookshelves, a fireplace, and an adjoining kitchen. Since the temperature rarely gets below fifty degrees in the winter, it's unusual for Keys homes to have fireplaces. But the old sea captain who built this place sixty years back had married a wealthy woman from Nova Scotia who loved cold weather. Promising her it got so bitter cold in the Keys during January and February, he assured her they would need a large fireplace. As the story goes, it was the first year, January 20, 1948, when she moved back to Canada.

Off to one side of the main Florida room is a large master bedroom and bath; to the other side is an office. Set up like a gem lab with scopes, refractometer, scales for weighing stones, polariscope, specific gravity liquids, black lights, and bookshelves full of information on gemology and stone identification, this is where I do all of the gemology work for Caribbean Jewelry. It is quiet, professional, and comfortable.

Downstairs, beneath all of this, are the garage and a tackle room for fly rods and reels with a large bench for tying flies.

But the best feature of the whole house is underneath the wooden deck behind the tackle room. The huge beams that support the upper deck also have stainless steel pulleys with cables and straps that hang below the beams down to the water. They hold my sixteen-foot Maverick skiff, one beam over the bow and one aft supporting the stern.

We threw a couple of fly rods in the skiff, lowered it with the cables, and were skidding across Cudjoe Bay in just a few minutes. The tide was rising in the backcountry which of course is the best tide for permit. So we decided to run out to the backside of the islands, the gulf side. We ran through Bow Channel along Johnson Keys and headed west about a mile. I cut the engine, climbed up on the poling platform, and began to pole us toward Barracuda Keys. It is here that the flats have a rocky coral ledge full of tasty crustaceans and little crabs. And on a full tide, it's a buffet for large, happy, tailing permit.

Limbo stood on the bow with my nine weight Scott rod, a large arbor loop reel, weight forward floating line, twelve-foot leader with ten-pound tippet, and a crab fly I probably tied a year ago. This felt good. I was in a good place for the moment and it was long overdue.

"Hey, Powell, this reel's on backwards." He laughed.

"Don't start," I answered.

It's a big debate among the fly-fishing gurus. Reel with your left hand, fight the fish with your strong arm, or reel faster with your strong hand. I say whatever you are used to, whatever works. I reel with my left hand; Limbo uses his right. But this fits with our continuous disputes about everything; everything from politics, music, and art to women, sex and drugs.

Now, as I look at the likable fool on the bow, I realized the only thing we do agree on is our friendship. And it will be that friendship we will both need to survive the nightmare we are about to experience.

I was beginning to feel guilty about fishing today. Although a bad storm was forming way down south, today was gorgeous. With the sun to our back, I was poling eastward with water visibility on the gulf side so transparent I could spot a fish a hundred yards away. And at this very moment, Dawn was in the hospital fighting for her life. Guilt!

Something subtly caught my attention. I scanned the area turning my head slightly to let the polarized lens in my sunglasses do their job.

"There!" I said, "Limbo, two o'clock, two hundred feet, a big silver flash." As I turned the skiff slightly, I now saw the fish. It was a pair of fine permit. They were feeding. And they were very happy. Limbo saw them now at eleven o'clock working their way toward us.

"Don't forget, the reel's on backwards," I softly said. "Try not to screw this up," I continued. Limbo was too focused to say anything, but I knew what he was thinking. It most likely included an F-word or two.

When the fish were about ninety feet from Limbo's toes, he started his back cast. Shooting line back and forth, his last forward shot landed the fly softly two feet in front of the smaller fish's nose. The fly sank to the bottom. Both fish saw the crab imitation at the exact moment. Limbo twitched the fly two inches. The two fish with heads down and big black tails out of the water dove toward the fly. A big white puff of mud, a screaming drag, and a pair of wakes slicing through the surface of the water in opposite directions made my knees wiggle. Limbo had hooked the smaller permit, still very nice despite the size difference. I could see the larger fish exit the flat into a deep channel two hundred yards out. Limbo's fish, about fifteen pounds, was all silver with a dark black dorsal fin and big black forked tail. Any permit caught on a fly is quite a feat, taking much skill and a bit of luck as well. Limbo's permit surprised us both. For a small fish, he had plenty of energy. He made a lightning first run out about a hundred and fifty yards. I heard Limbo mutter some

Corbett A. Davis Jr.

colorful utterance that of course included his favorite F-verb. It was about the same instant that the fish made his second run when the handle on the reel hit hard on Limbo's knuckles reminding him that the reel was left-hand retrieve.

"You want me to reel that fish in for you Limbo," I said, chuckling. More colorful verbs directed my way.

The permit, now very tired, changed his strategy. Too tired and worn down to make another long run, he turned his big flat body broadside, stuck his nose down into the coral bottom, and tried to snap the fly from his lip. He was not giving up easily but neither was Limbo. Any slack line and this fish would have spit the hook and joined his lucky buddy in the deep channel. It was not long before Limbo had his prize catch beside the boat. I carefully grabbed him in front of his tail, removed the barbless hook, and moved the tired fish back and forth into the current forcing fresh water through his gills. A few minutes later the revived fish sped off toward deep water. I jumped down off the poling platform and met Limbo on the bow of the skiff with a congratulatory high five.

It was my turn to fish, but I decided to just drift quietly along the flat, sipped on a Bud Light, and talk with Limbo. I grabbed a beer out of the cooler and flipped an O'Doul's over to Limbo.

To the south, evidence of a bad storm loomed in the heavens. Huge cumulus clouds drifted northward toward the Keys. And to the west, the sun, only two hours before setting, was for the moment amidst very clear skies.

Limbo sat on the bow facing me and the back of the skiff. He was barefoot and shirtless. Beneath his long-billed cap and sunglasses, there hung from his leathery neck a long gold twenty-four-inch chain weighing more than two ounces. And dangling from it was an unusual pendant that I had made at his request. It was an 18k yellow gold shark's jaws two inches high and an inch wide surrounding a heavy platinum St. Christopher with a child on his shoulder. He had told me that one day he would explain it. So far, he hadn't.

As we talked about fishing, women, the Keys, and our lives, I noticed something frightening that alarmed me. On both of Limbo's ears, his nose, and across his chest were numerous little scars. I was about to ask him about them, but he started nervously talking about something else, causing me to be distracted.

Later, when I thought about this, I felt like maybe he could read the concern in my eyes and didn't want to go there.

"Powell, you ever worry about making a big mistake?" Limbo asked.

"I never really thought about it, but I try not to make mistakes if I can help it," I replied. "Where'd that come from Limbo, what's up?" I asked.

"Oh, I don't know, just been thinking some crazy shit lately," he replied.

The tide was falling now and we were drifting more toward the east. It was calm, clear, and quiet. A pair of cormorants was taking turns diving down beneath the glassy surface mooching in a stingray's wake, looking for any food the ray's wings uncovered. An osprey was whistling loudly in the distance. A lone frigate bird circled high above us riding the wind currents. Nestled between a few puffy clouds, the bird's large black outline looked like the Bat-signal that meant trouble in Gotham City. Obviously, my mind was drifting also. Just when the vision of Dawn returned to my thoughts, Limbo broke the silence and said, "It's like Toby Keith says in that song with Buffett. We're best known for our big mistake!"

"What?" I said.

"Okay, Powell, let me ask you, who was Benedict Arnold?"

"A *traitor!*" I snapped.

"Yeah, that's all you know about him, huh?" Limbo asked with a grin. "Did you know that after the first three years of the Revolutionary War George Washington said Benedict Arnold was the most patriotic and bravest soldier on the battlefield?"

"So what?" I yelled.

"After being wounded twice in battle, Benedict Arnold captured Fort Ticonderoga, invaded Canada, and was the victor at the Battle of Saratoga," Limbo continued.

"Like I said, Limbo, so what, who gives a rat's ass?"

"Powell, if you fuck up, do you want to be remembered for your one big mistake?"

"No, I guess not," I said. "By the way, why do you listen to Buffett's new music? It sucks! Stick to his old albums Limbo."

"You're wrong, Powell. His new music is where it's at, with much more meaning and thought. He's a genius," Limbo said abruptly.

"Limbo, you're old and full of shit. His old music had feeling and described a way of life. He gave in and did exactly what he said he'd never do. He's making music for money now, so who's going to make music for me?"

"Maybe Justin Bieber would be more your style. Powell, you're young and fucked up!" Limbo snapped.

It was how all of our arguments went. He loved the new sounds, particularly Latin music and even hip-hop. I liked the old Buffett, Allman Brothers, and Dylan. He was liberal. I was conservative. He was old, and I was young. He was agnostic, maybe even atheist. I'm Catholic since birth. And yet we were friends, friends that argued, but definitely friends.

"Hey, Limbo, do me a favor. Quit throwing the F-word around so much. I mean really now, what's up with that? I'm starting to use it as much as you do. And I don't want to do that. Okay?" I asked.

"Okay, you pussy," he said as we both got a good belly laugh.

CHAPTER 9

Dawn's naked body lied still beneath a thin, sheer sheet. Even unconscious, her beauty was extraordinary. They had removed her clothes and all of her jewelry except for a pair of platinum diamond stud earrings. Her physique was frail yet still gorgeous, voluptuous, and very sexy. Her blonde hair had been washed and blown dry. With firm round breasts, perfectly sized nipples, long slim legs, and a flat stomach, Dawn Landry had a body to die for or rather, in her case, to kill for.

Although her beautiful form is not what they were after, it would keep her alive at least for the moment. But soon, she would have to die. Dawn's inner beauty of heart and soul had brought her here. Actually, it was her heart and other vital organs, such as kidneys, lungs, and liver. Dawn's rare allure was not just skin deep. She also had a very rare blood type, AB Rh negative, which only about five percent of all humans on Earth had running through their veins. Dawn had inherited her mother's piercingly exquisite *azul* eyes and also one gene of her AB positive blood. From her father's side, she was fortunate enough to get his smooth dark complexion but was cursed enough to inherit the negative gene of his O negative blood. And whether bad luck or fate, Dawn had the same blood type as the only son of the Shah of Iran.

The Shah of Iran and his family were all of Muslim descent and followed Islam. When his twenty-year-old son became ill and needed a new heart, the Shah demanded research on AB negative blood types and ordered samples from everyone near him. He was convinced that

Rh-negative blood was much more than just a mere blood type. He claimed, based on Koran, that Rh-negative blood originated from guardian angels that interbred with human women before the ocean gushed water. That is how Muslims and the Koran described the disastrous flood. The speculation continued that the Rh-negative genes passed on to Noah and the postflood civilization. Although the Shah did not recognize Jesus as Lord, he did believe that the blood of Jesus was AB negative based on evidence of the shroud. He also believed that recent UFO sightings were actually the watcher angels who were bestowed the same blood type as his son, Jesus, and a beautiful young organ donor from Key West, Florida, by the name of Dawn Landry.

Dawn heard a voice. Sensing trouble, she carefully squinted through one eye. A young Mideastern man, well dressed with a full beard and wearing a doctor's smock, leaned over and held a stethoscope to her chest. The surprisingly cold metal made her flinch. The young doctor stepped back and watched her for a moment. Her breathing was slow and calm. He continued to examine Dawn's body and listened to the blood flow in her delicate arteries and veins. The internal rhythmic sounds signified a strong and steady heartbeat. "Perfect!" he thought aloud.

Dawn heard no other sounds. Her bruised mind thought that to be odd. No PA announcements, no music, no other patients, and no staff. What kind of hospital is this, she thought. She felt pain at her ankles and wrists. Dawn tried to move her legs then her arms. It was at that moment when she realized she was restrained.

Dr. Shezad glanced at the commercial cable ties that held Dawn's body stationary. She was like a goddess lying there on the table, completely nude, completely vulnerable. He, for a brief moment, considered whether to undress and mount her, force himself inside her, and satisfy his sudden insatiable craving. Her legs were spread and bound and her body was naked. She was there for the taking. He was aroused, hard, and ready.

Dawn felt his stare and somehow knew his thoughts. She clinched her teeth; her body was tight and rigid. She would not lay still and let this happen. Dawn was ready to fight and die if necessary. She held her breath and tried to focus her thoughts elsewhere.

Shezad kissed her cheek, working his way down, next her jawline, down her neck, stopping at her chest. He took a moment adoring her breasts, licking, pinching, and biting her nipples. Dawn knew if she was to survive she had to be calm and almost comatose. It was getting more and more difficult.

The young intern was now kissing her belly, his hands caressing her thighs. And finally, his face hovered above her. Dawn felt his breath between her legs. Disgusted and nauseous, she could no longer lie still. Just as Dawn was about to scream, writhing from discomfort, someone entered the room and grabbed the doctor around the throat. Unknowingly, she opened her eyes and tried her best to wriggle free from the constraints. Luckily, her movements were unnoticed. She heard a deep, accented voice yell, "I told you not to touch her. She is holy!"

Next, Dawn heard a loud and disturbing crack, then silence, total eerie silence. It was muteness, a quiet that only comes from the sounds of a neck breaking. She felt herself sobbing internally but refused to show emotion. She was holy and had to survive this until Powell could rescue her and return to their once happy lives.

She felt a burn in her right arm, heard water splash, and then a dark abyss swept over her once again.

Corbett A. Davis Jr.

CHAPTER 10

After catching Limbo's permit, we had been afloat for a good part of the afternoon. Limbo and I had discussed issues, had argued about nothing and had laughed and even cried. I wasn't sure what he had on his mind, but I was certain something bad or evil preoccupied Limbo's brain.

"You okay, Limbo?" I asked.

"Sure Powell, what could be wrong on a day like this?" he answered.

"Powell, you ever think of what you would do if you only had a few months to live?"

I thought it a very odd question and frankly a little unnerving. I tried not to show my concern.

"Not really, but I guess I would tie up loose ends and spend time with my family and friends. You know, tell them good-bye and let them know I love them and appreciate all they have done for me in my life. Confess my sins. Then, if I were able, Dawn and I would travel the ocean. Hit every little island in the Caribbean. Live on love, lobster, and what little luck I had left," I said.

The fact is I'm not sure what I would do. Maybe I'd write a book, a good-bye for my family to remember me by. Some little part of me they would always have and feel. The worse thing is to be forgotten. I want to be remembered for who I am and for the good that I brought to someone's life. Maybe that's what Limbo was getting at. Not being known for our one big mistake. My mind was skipping around, out of control. I collected my thoughts, calmed my nerves, and asked Limbo, "So what would you do in that situation, knowing you only had a few months to live?"

"Well, Powell, believe it or not, I have thought about that quite a bit lately."

I did not like where this was going. I felt like I was about to hear some hidden, dark, personal secret in Limbo's life. Being good friends, I thought I knew him well but all day he had been distant. Had something happened in the past few months when we were out of touch? And did I want to know about it if it had? Many things popped into my head but nothing like what he was about to tell me.

"Powell, I know exactly what I would do if I only had a few months to live. I would find the person I hated most on this Earth, and I would kill her. It would be a slow death and painful death. And I would not regret it, not for one moment."

Her? I felt a little weak and sickened. We said nothing else. We drifted eastward, slowly toward Sawyer Key.

The beauty of a spectacular sunset was lost from the strain of conversation. As if in a coma, I stared in wonder at the big orange ball as it was consumed by the mangroves on the horizon. It was swallowed up in an instant, a flash my eye just missed. Like the fly in our permit's jaw, it was sucked down quickly, putting a close to what could have been a perfect day.

Corbett A. Davis Jr.

CHAPTER 11

The weather had completely deteriorated by the time we decided to head the skiff back to Cudjoe Key. Limbo was quiet. I wondered what was going on in that confused head of his. Maybe he wished he had kept his mouth shut, or maybe he was thinking of his human target. I had many questions filling my cerebral lobe as I tried to hold steady and maneuver the skiff through thunderstorms saturated with rain and lightning.

Why all the scars on Limbo's face, nose, and ears? Who in the world could Limbo hate enough to kill? What was the meaning behind that shark jaws St. Christopher necklace? These were all important questions but obviously questions that would only be answered when Limbo was ready to talk. I only hoped he would open up and talk to me before he did something he might regret.

The sky darkened quickly. The cloud cover was so thick that there was not even a hint of sunshine to be found. There were no stars. The winds were beginning to pick up. Extreme bad weather had been forecast. Late night predictions included tropical storm warnings with wind gusts up to ninety miles per hour. Offshore waves were expected to reach fifteen feet while inside the reef would see six to eight feet seas. Small craft warnings were already in effect and would continue through Saturday.

I finally got the Maverick in the boat slip after running thirty minutes in the storm with twenty-knot winds. Limbo and I were soaking wet and shivering form the cold.

Looking south out across the ocean, I realized the storm was approaching quickly. I knew Limbo would be stuck here, unable to escape the weather and my questions. A bolt of lightning created a halo of orange fire that surrounded total darkness out across the sea. It was disturbed darkness filled with the pandemonium of disorderly, unpredictable winds along with confused seas. Mountainous clouds spewed lighting in every direction like molten lava from a volcano. The Atlantic sea breeze turned tornadic as the winds moved inside the reef sucking the oxygen right out of the dense atmosphere. My mind's vision, now in hurricane mode, conjured thoughts of numerous water spouts poking holes in the turbulent surf with water spinning at the base like my mother's old Maytag. My only sense of direction came from the sound of violent disoriented white caps crashing along the eastern shore of Cudjoe Bay.

As if in a choreographed light show from the heavens accompanied by a background of thunderous skies, deadly squalls collided as violently and destructively as my own life's present course. Hopefully, my problems would subside as quickly as the forecast predictions for this infernal storm.

As much as I hoped that Dawn would soon join me in my efforts to salvage my life, I feared deeply that she was never going to return. There were no exact reasons for this conclusion, only a nagging gut feeling. I've always believed in karma, more recently described as "what goes around, comes around!" Bad karma had taken control over my life, and I was heading for a collision with self-destruction. My business had suffered, Dawn had left me, and now, Limbo was rationalizing murder. I needed to change my destiny as soon as possible. It's fourth and twenty. My team is down by two touchdowns, and there is not much time left on the clock. I have to change the momentum, turn the tides, and find enough determination to put some points back on the scoreboard.

Corbett A. Davis Jr.

The storm's fury had now settled in as if targeting Cudjoe Bay. My thoughts swirled in as many directions as the wind outside that now was piercing the banana leaves and palm fronds. It was time to face my demons and excommunicate the evil that has inhabited my body for the past couple of years.

For a moment, my distorted gray matter tried to shift to something more pleasant. I shamelessly caught myself daydreaming of a young girl from Mobile Alabama that loved to fly-fish and had blue eyes the color of the Gulf Stream. I quickly forced Tracy from my thoughts, wondering how Dawn was doing tonight. To rid myself of momentary guilt, I focused once again to check on the girl of my dreams and more recently, my nightmares.

While Limbo showered, I called Dawn. The same nurse answered with the same results. Now I couldn't see Dawn until 11:00 a.m. tomorrow and not a second before. She was still in ICU and could not come to the phone. No wonder they all love their damn jobs so much, I thought. They're all a bunch of insensitive assholes!

I would deal with them tomorrow morning, but first things first. My recipe for recovery included an early run to get this abused body back into shape. Afterward, I would go by the jewelry store and access the damage of my neglect. I would do all of this early enough to be at Seaman's Hospital at 11:00 a.m. sharp to rescue Dawn from the uncaring and rude staff.

But tonight, I had a much bigger task.

CHAPTER 12

The violent storm still raged on. Coconuts were being tossed around the yard like baseballs shot out of a pitching machine. Every few minutes one would pummel into the side of the house or thrash the water below the deck. The sounds were alarming and distracting, but I knew what I had to do. It was time to talk seriously to Limbo and help him deal with his demons.

I needed to help him, not just for his welfare but also more importantly for my own peace of mind. It would help on my personal road to recovery as I tried to rebound from nearly two years of self-destruction.

After his shower, Limbo burst into the room with only a towel wrapped around his waist, making quite an unusual entrance. His unkempt hair was still wet, and the tan hide on his back and shoulders were the color of burnt pine bark. Scars and blemishes covering his skin like a jigsaw puzzle were evidence of too many hours blistering in the sun. His thinning blonde hair showed a solar abused scalp with similar markings.

Looking out of a large picture window facing due south, I had a spectacular view of a squall churning over Cudjoe Bay. I have two Adirondack indoor teak chairs there, and I sat in one as Limbo plopped his wet ass in the other. His aimless stare concerned me. His earlier remarks concerned me. Hell, his appearance scared the shit out of me. Just when I was deciding how I would start the discussion, he abruptly spoke. Out of his mouth came words I never expected. It caught me so off guard I'm sure he saw my jaw drop. But it also opened the door for serious conversation.

"You got any rum, Powell?" Limbo asked.

"Are you shitting me?" I replied. "You haven't had a drink in what? Twenty-five years?" I continued.

"So what, Powell? What's the worst that could happen? It would kill me? I really don't have to worry much about that anymore," he said as a bolt of lightning lit up the room revealing a very solemn yet peaceful expression on Limbo's face. We sat in silence for a couple of minutes as I collected my thoughts and stared out over the water.

Finally, I said, a bit too loudly, "What gives, Limbo? What the hell is going on? You're going to have to talk to me. You've been letting yourself fall apart physically, you're talking about wanting to kill someone, you're way too secretive about things, and now for god's sake, you think you need a drink after twenty-five years!"

Limbo slowly stood up, not saying a word, and walked to my liquor cabinet. He pulled out a bottle of Mount Gay Rum, grabbed a tall glass, got a couple of ice cubes from the refrigerator door, and overfilled the glass, spilling it on the tile floor. He smiled, removed the towel from his waist, and wiped up the rum leaving the towel draped across the kitchen floor. It was a bizarre sight as he walked back across the room to his chair, bolts of lightning exposing his naked body. I probably looked like I had seen a zombie. He sat and drank slowly from the glass. The only sounds heard were from the thunder of the nearby squall. I didn't know what to say so I remained speechless as quiet as a kid in a confessional waiting for the priest's window to slide open. Limbo consumed most of the drink and then turned, looked me in the eye and said, "Powell, the doctors tell me I probably won't live to see my sixtieth birthday."

I felt my lungs collapse, forcing the air from my throat, leaving me light headed and nauseous. I hoped I had misunderstood because I knew that Limbo's sixtieth was less than two months away. I felt myself in a fog hovering above looking down at two dreadful souls, me self-destructing and Limbo motionless, buck naked, and dying. I wanted to say something but the words would not come. Limbo turned and muttered something that was somewhat muted by thunder. From my blank look and eyes that bulged as big as a Volkswagen's headlights, he realized his message was not heard. Limbo repeated just one word.

"Cancer!" he said loud enough to be heard over the storm.

Before I could respond and probably meaning it to be that way, Limbo began speaking.

It would be a sad but incredible story, a story that would explain all of his inner demons and devils.

"After working with the CIA and U.S. Customs for so many years Powell, I've made a few enemies. About seven years ago, I had just finished working a disturbing undercover murder case involving some Columbian drug lords and a ruthless woman real estate developer by the name of Everset DeMilo."

Limbo stopped long enough to fill his glass again with rum. This time he added the juice of two key limes he found on the counter next to the refrigerator. He laughed loudly when he looked down, realizing for the first time he was naked.

"Where was I?" he said. "Oh yes, Eve Knight, Mrs. DeMilo's favorite alias. Well, U.S. Customs had followed the money trail that Eve left behind, all the way south to Vieques, Puerto Rico. When her banker, attorney, and husband were all three found floating tits up in a local lagoon with their throats slit, I was called in to investigate."

I was all ears like a school kid sitting on his grandfather's knee at story-telling time. Although I always suspected it, this was the first time Limbo ever openly admitted working with the CIA or Customs. I hoped I would hear the whole account before he passed out from a rum overdose.

Captain Limbo continued, "Well, Powell, to make a long story short, I spent two months in Vieques undercover as a fishing guide investigating Eve and her two Columbian drug lord partners. The golf and dive resort she was developing in Puerto Rico was nothing more than a way to launder money. It was the perfect plan. Her private resort had a huge marina with an entrance completely hidden among the Mangrove trees. Boats would come and go, load cocaine, and unload cash. The Columbians furnished the drugs while illegal Cubans from Tampa Florida paid and transported the booty to Everglades City on the west side of the glades near Marco Island."

"So, Limbo," I interrupted, "does any of this have anything to do with that bizarre necklace hanging around your neck? You have to admit pal, a platinum and gold set of shark jaws with St. Christopher suspended in the bull sharks maw the size of a silver dollar is a bit peculiar."

"Right?" I added.

I felt like I was just babbling to hear myself talk. As much as I wanted and needed to understand this conversation, it was unsettling. My friend was in trouble, and I wanted to help, but his talk of death, murder, and now confession was overwhelming.

Limbo's dismal gaze pierced my body and psyche as if he had not heard a word I muttered.

"Can I finish now, Powell?" he snapped.

I just nodded.

"As a guide fishing out of her marina, I was able to get close and very familiar with all of the players. At one point, one of the Columbians even jokingly hinted around offering me a job. I always thought it was just a test to see if I would take the bait, which, of course, I did. After a few more weeks of guiding clients for Eve DeMilo, I noticed that her demeanor changed dramatically. Or maybe I was just being paranoid as a result of what I had learned about her and her ruthless partners. One Sunday, she called and summoned me to have brunch with her and the two Columbian partners. It was a very calm and hot summer day. Not a breath of air was blowing when we sat down at her outdoor waterfront marina café. I ate my conch salad slowly not looking up as she spoke. Out of the corner of my eye, I focused on the body language, movements, and expressions of the two thugs sitting with us. And, Powell, I have to say, the hair on the back of my neck felt like I was in an electrical storm. When I took a sip of my Medalla Cerveza, I made eye contact with of one of the Columbians. I should have known at that very moment that nothing good would come of this lunch.

"Like a fool, I agreed to meet them at their boat the next morning at four o'clock. I acted grateful and overjoyed at the twenty-five thousand dollar bonus they offered for my services. I felt like I would have won the Oscar at the Academy Awards if they had a category for the best actor in an illegal scenario. After six months, they finally trusted me, or did they? From the suspicious maddening glare I saw in ole Gomez's eye, I wasn't sure.

"Morning came too soon and brought not only a stiff fifteen-knot wind but also a cloud covering that resulted in an eerie pitch-black darkness I would never forget. The plan was to rendezvous with Gomez's cousin forty miles offshore just before the early light of sunrise exposed us to the world. We would load the drugs onto the Bertram Sportfisher quickly and then slowly fish our way back to the docks. This did two

Corbett A. Davis Jr.

things. Not only did it give the guise of fishing but also delayed our return to the marina until after the sun set."

I grabbed Limbo's empty glass, went to the kitchen made us both a very large Cuba libre with fresh key lime juice and sat back down. I said, "So you were drinking Medalla Cerveza huh? Limbo I think we both need a tall stiff drink!"

Limbo smiled and said, "Yeah, Powell, I was drinking beer again by then. Relax, try not to worry about it. Besides, do you remember what Benjamin Franklin used to say?"

I shrugged my shoulders. "No, what did Ben have to say."

"He said that beer is proof that God loves us and wants us to be happy."

Limbo smiled, took a big sip of rum, and continued.

"It was about noon while we slowly drifted the Gulf Stream using live bait when the shit hit the fan. Gomez and Rodriguez, or whatever the hell their names, were had been chumming with bloody bonito, hard tails, and mackerel for hours. They said they were trying to raise snapper and grouper to the surface to catch."

"And Powell, just as you know from all of your years on the water, chumming bloody fish chunks does not attract snapper and grouper. However, as I watched off the stern of the boat, I counted at least six different species of sharks as they thrashed through the bloody waters."

"Then, Powell, my worst fear was confirmed when one of the Columbian guerillas asked me, 'What you think your buddies at Customs or the CIA would think about this kind of fishing?' Their laugh, in unison, was sinister and uncomfortable to say the least.

"I knew I was in trouble!"

Limbo's expression was vacant, void of all meaning. I thought maybe I should not have pushed so hard for an explanation. However, there was no way he wasn't going to get this off his chest. He wanted to tell the story. He needed me to know. I felt like closure for him was necessary, but I would not let myself dwell on the reasons why. That could prove to be uncomfortable and frightening. Listening to Limbo's description of the entire account and knowing from his sincerity the tale was factual made it difficult to understand how he ever lived to talk about it.

When Limbo yelled, "Are you listening to me, Powell?"

I jumped and nodded though actually I wasn't really listening. I was caught up deep in my own mind horrified with thoughts of his danger and his fear, which caused me anxiety. I heard loud, slow breaths of air inhaled and exhaled. It was my own breathing I listened to.

"Yeah! I hear you, Limbo," I calmly replied.

"How the hell did you get out of that situation?" I added.

"Well, Powell," Limbo started. "I quickly scanned the boat, the Columbians and the sharks. It's funny how one's body reacts after such a close observation surveyance. My senses sharpened. I saw body language, movement, and concern. I heard their thoughts and plans, but I also heard the splashing of the water from dozens of huge sharks that were now in a frenzy as deadly scavengers hunting for food. They were a perfect eating machine as Captain Quint would refer to them in the *Jaws* movies. Suddenly, I felt Gomez in my face as his accomplice circled around behind me. Alerted by fright and adrenaline, my older and slower keen senses spread to my reflexes. For no reason, I dropped to one knee as I spun around kicking the legs out from under the Columbian. His head hit the gunnel creating a loud thud. Blood spewed from the open wound like crude oil from a newly tapped well. He quickly stood, keeping my attention a moment too long. Gomez reacted. His muscular arms had my neck gripped like an egg in a vise. The other Columbian, very pissed off now, was coming at me with vengeance in his eyes. Blood still spilling

Corbett A. Davis Jr.

from his head, it did not seem to slow his pace or divert his anger. The hold on my throat now cut off air. My windpipe was kinked like a twisted water hose. I felt the blood rush from my head, leaving me dazed. I knew I had to react. I remembered a large gaff stowed under the starboard gunnel. The only chance for my survival was to work myself towards it. My head was now full of fog, and my eyes could not focus. Gomez still had the grip of a bench vise cutting off all oxygen. The other Columbian was coming at me with his fist cocked. His face was covered with clots of blood. His black hair stuck to the coagulating dark maroon fluid. I knew he had lost a lot of blood, but by the time he bled out, I would be shark shit."

"You have a way with words, Limbo," I said just to get a breath of fresh air. As I fixed us two more very tall rum and Cokes, Limbo finished the story.

"Gomez was lifting my body now trying to get me over the side. Thank God it was the starboard side. My right hand blindly searched below the gunnel, finding the six-foot gaff. As one Columbian lifted me by the neck, the other was sprawled out reaching for my legs. With the last bit of energy I had left in my body, I sunk the gaff into the Columbian's torso. His piercing shriek startled Gomez for a split instant, allowing an unexpected release of pressure around my neck. It was just long enough for me to gasp, fill my lungs full of air, lift the gaff up, and throw it overboard. The Columbian was still attached.

CHAPTER 13

Before Gomez's compadre hit the surface, the blue waters beneath him were filled with gray fins, instinct and hunger which are a deadly combination in such animals.

Gomez held his tight grip on my vocal cords. Although I could not see what was happening in the water, I could feel it and hear it."

Limbo stopped for a minute. Then, looking as if he had just relived the drama, he continued.

"Powell, the sounds I heard that day were straight from hell. The first bull shark was the devil himself ripping at the Columbian's flesh, dragging him deeper and deeper as the other bull sharks, tigers, lemons, and hammerheads fought for their share." I pictured the shark with his gnashing jaws, swimming into an abyss, past purgatory, into a bottomless pit of an infernal region where the fires of hell would have been a blessing had he made it. Which of course he did not. "Powell, you probably didn't realize it, but there are only about sixty to seventy shark attacks in the world each year. And it is quite rare that the attacks are fatal. Well, ole Jose here surely screwed up that statistic."

"So Limbo, did you throw Gomez overboard too?" I asked.

"No, not exactly," Limbo said.

"Gomez was pretty shaken up by the sight of his amigo's brutal death, and that once again caused him to release pressure on my neck. I took advantage of the moment. As soon as I could gasp for air, I elbowed him in the gut, pulled free from his hold, and hit him as hard as I could between the eyes. He fell backwards, but I also stumbled. The stranglehold had taken its toll. I was on my knees trying to breathe and think, but he recovered before I was able to. Gomez was pissed. One eye was swollen shut from an encounter with my fist. The other was wide-open, wild, opaque, and wanting revenge. That's when I first saw the spear gun."

"Limbo, are you making this shit up?" I finally asked. He didn't see the humor in my question.

Limbo continued, "He had it aimed at my chest and all four rubbers on the gun were cocked and loaded. Knowing how accurate and powerful a band-powered spear gun can be, I made the only choice I could. It was not an option to stay and fight. I would have been no match for the spear. I jumped up ran to the port gunnel and dove headfirst overboard. Realizing my chances of surviving the sharks were only slightly better than the spear gun, I still knew it was my only alternative. Trying to stay calm and not thrash in the water, I looked around. I could occasionally see a flash of silver, down very deep. I knew exactly what was going on at that depth but tried hard to not think about it or panic. I was about at my limit of holding my breath when I felt something shoot past my leg. I looked down and immediately recognized the spear that I had seen aimed at my head earlier. I reached, grabbed, and yanked it in one fast motion. It must have caught Gomez off guard because I ripped it right out of his hand."

Limbo paused again. I could see the anguish in his face and was beginning to feel the hatred he had for Gomez and Everset DeMilo. I didn't speak.

Limbo finally did.

"I swam up to the bow of the boat under the v-hull and surfaced. Gomez had no way of knowing where I was. Hidden from sight, I kept still hoping that school of frenzied sharks had drifted with the strong current and what would be left of the Columbian. Then, as if music from the heavens, I heard the two diesel engines fire up. I wondered if Gomez thought the sharks got me or maybe that the spear pierced my heart as it tore away from his hands. I didn't care. He was leaving. I took a huge gulp of air and dove down as deep as I could. About fifteen feet down, I realized I still gripped the stainless steel spear in my right hand. I tried to relax and stay calm to keep my heart rate as slow as possible. I needed Gomez to put the boat in gear and leave soon, real soon. Although there is substantiated evidence of a Swiss free diver who had held his breath for over nineteen minutes, it would be pure luck if I were to make it two minutes under water. I had already been down close to that. My body was deprived of precious oxygen. It was only a matter of time that the carbon dioxide levels would build, triggering a reflex that would cause my diaphragm and muscles around my ribs to spasm.

I heard the roar of the engine and could see the boat's following wake leaving above. I swam for the surface. Powell, when we hold our breath underwater, luckily we have mammalian evolution on our side. Our bodies instinctively prepare to conserve oxygen, our heart rate drops, blood pressure goes up, and circulation redistributes that oxygen to our vital organs.

It was about two minutes and fifteen seconds when I came out of the water, shooting toward the sky like a killer whale at Sea World. Gomez was already a small speck in the distance. My relief and happiness disappeared as quickly as Gomez's sport fisherman had. I was forty miles offshore adrift all alone in shark-infested waters.

For the first three hours, I dog-paddled with the cocked spear gun. Every few minutes, I would stick my head beneath the surface and search for sharks. By nightfall, I was weary, hungry, and very thirsty. My mind began to wander, drift, and play games. I sang songs, thought aloud, and even prayed."

"You prayed?" I interrupted. "I thought you were an atheist, Limbo?"

With concern, Limbo glanced my way and said, "I thought I'd cover all the bases, Powell. In fact, that was the night I started my own church. I was the pastor, the congregation, the holy and the unholy. I named my new church 'The Church of Just in Case.' I prayed all night, not sure to whom but I knew that sharks prefer to feed at dusk, dark, and dawn. Just before sunrise, I saw the first dorsal fin. It was a lemon shark about eight feet long. I lay on the surface as still as a drifting log. He swam over, nudged my hip with his nose, and slowly swam away. I didn't realize it, but I was holding my breath again. I exhaled loudly. To keep my mind busy, I tried to think of everything I knew about lemon sharks. Noticing that I had drifted into a large sargasso weed patch, for some reason, I felt some comfort I was partially hidden from sight. Lemon sharks like tropical waters. If my memory is correct, the longest one ever caught was thirteen feet long, and they usually have remoras attached. I was floating in the Gulf Stream, a powerful, warm, and swift river that flows easterly and northerly.

"Powell, I remember thinking that the Gulf Stream was the river Billy Joel sang about. 'The River of Dreams' had to be where this newly ordained pastor of the first, holy 'Church of Just in Case' now floated about like a note in a bottle. As I drifted with the sargasso weed, I kept my eyes closed. The sun had taken its toll on my body. My forehead, arms, and shoulders were blistered. I felt something carved into the wooden stock on the spear gun, so I forced an eye open to look. GCH was scratched into the wood. I decided to decipher the code in order to keep my mind working. Someone would see me soon. Who was I kidding? Was I losing what little mind I had left? Great Country Ham?

Good Chick Hunting? God's Cold Heart? Good Children Hide? I was dehydrated, burned by the sun, and not in a good place mentally. I thought of the Indian phrase, 'Today is a good day to die!' But I did not want to die today. I was not a brave warrior. I did not deserve to die an honorable death today.

"When I first heard the hum, I thought it was in my head, a noise between my sunburned ears. My eyes would hardly open now. Again, I forced one open. Fishing and following the weed line, I saw the most beautiful Hatteras I'd ever seen. And better yet, they saw me."

"Wow! That is an amazing story Limbo. You are one lucky SOB!"

I continued, "No wonder you wear that thing around your neck!"

"I thought that might clear it up for you, Powell!" The jaws are for the eight foot lemon shark that kissed my ass and although the Catholic de-sainted him, St. Christopher is now the patron saint of the 'Church of Just in Case.' It's my good luck charm. I was fortunate that day, Powell. I found out three weeks later after I had fully recovered that ole Gomez thought he had hit me with the spear gun. He assumed that I drowned and sank to the bottom since I never surfaced."

"Now how do you know that, Limbo?" I asked with slight skepticism in my voice.

"Because he told me that himself," Limbo replied.

"You see, I made another visit to Vieques and found Gomez out at his secluded home on the ocean. He was sitting by the pool when I startled him with my unexpected arrival. The visit was brief. We had a short chat, and that is when he told me that he assumed I died at sea that day. Gomez was very sorry for his sins and begged forgiveness. Actually, it was the first confession I've heard as pastor of the new church," Limbo said with a huge grin.

Corbett A. Davis Jr.

The sun was about to rise across Cudjoe Bay. Normally, I would have been so tired I couldn't keep my eyes open but not tonight, not this night.

Limbo finished, "The next day, news made the *Miami Herald*. Front page, top story was of interest to many Americans, especially myself. 'Real estate developer and businessman Gomez Carlos Henriques Dies Tragic Death.' Ruled an accident, Gomez was found in his pool dressed in his wet suit and diving gear. They say he accidently shot himself. The spear entered below his chin and came out through the top of his head. They ruled out any foul play because his mishap resulted from shooting himself with his own spear gun. It even had his initials carved in the handle. GCH, Gomez Carlos Henriques."

CHAPTER 14

Powell Taylor had a very restless evening, especially considering the troubling story Limbo had just purged and shared from his past. Powell seemed to get the same satisfaction and peace hearing a confession as he remembered getting so long ago when he would visit the confessional himself. The murders concerned Powell, but he opted to believe it was all in self-defense. There were many questions still to ask but not today. Powell was feeling good. He could see Dawn soon. He understood Limbo a little better now, and it was a glorious sunny South Florida kind of day on Cudjoe Key. He made a pot of Cuban coffee and slipped outside to pick up his copy of the *Key West Times* from the dew-drenched grass. All he was interested in was the weather report. Powell tossed the paper on his chair out on the back deck and returned to the kitchen to pour himself a large cup of his favorite brew.

Key West was bustling early. Tourists were crammed on Duval Street. Parasailors filled the sky, sportfishers trolled the reef, and dive flags littered the gulf. The bars and restaurants were crowded and loud. The music from Sloppy Joes melted into the tunes coming from Captain Tony's. The conch train still snaked through the streets of old Key West filled with an array of colorful bermuda shorts and pink skin slathered with sunscreen. The Hemingway House tour had a line two blocks long. New Jerseyans hoped to see the legendary six- and seven-toed cats along with other memorabilia and mementoes left by Ernest Hemingway. On one bookshelf was a gift from Picasso, a colorful cat fashioned out of clay.

Above the shelf on the wall was a framed quote that some say is just as bogus as Hemingway having cats when he lived here. Ernest's second wife, Pauline, had found the house in 1931. Her Uncle Gus bought it for eight thousand dollars and gave it to the newlyweds as a wedding gift. It was here that Ernest Hemingway completed *A Farewell to Arms*. Most say it was the torturous hot days of August without air-conditioning that prompted Ernest to recite the quote now hanging on the wall that reads, "I'd rather eat monkey shit than die in Key West!"

Maybe had he stayed in Key West, his life would have been prolonged.

Down on Mallory Square, the hustle and bustle had started before the sun came up. Key West was truly alive today, so much so that no one even noticed what was missing. *Lady Demonio* had left the harbor sometime during the early hours of darkness. She was now ten miles offshore, headed south-southwest on a course of 202 degrees direct to Marina Hemingway in Havana. For a beautiful sunny day, the winds were unusually strong and the seas reached eight to ten feet in the Gulf Stream. The cursed ship bounced and tossed in the rolling seas like a kayak in the surf. Still bound and tied at the wrists and ankles, Dawn Landry was becoming nauseous from the turbulent motion.

CHAPTER 15

I took a sip of hot, dark-roasted Bustelo coffee; sat down on the back deck; and picked up the paper. My joyous mood collapsed instantly. The front-page headline grabbed me like a wind-thrown treble hook coming to rest in the side of my neck. Just below the *Key West Times* familiar logo it read, "Total count of decimated bodies reaches twenty-one."

As much as I wanted to call Limbo and ask his opinion about the story, daylight was near, and time was wasting. I had things to do. Today, my road to recovery begins. And it most definitely would be a difficult journey. I looked at the pathetic list hanging on the front of my refrigerator that I had written in my drunken stupor. It was time to work on number 3, exercise and get into shape. Hopefully, numbers one and two would follow easily.

I put the newspaper by the phone where later I would study it and call Limbo.

The vision of my foul reflection in the bathroom mirror at Coco's Cantina that night now returned vividly and filled my thoughts. It was that moment when I realized just how low I had let myself fall. That horrid and repulsive memory haunted me as I tied the laces of my new Nike running shoes. It was time to regain my health and redeem myself from this undesirable condition. Getting physically fit surely would help my mental existence. Both body and mind were desperately in need of sound readiness. A good run was the first step. Although the sun had not risen, the temperature had already reached the mideighties. I hoped the sweat pouring from my bulging body would purge the poison that filled my pores. I had a plan that consisted of a healthy diet and some exercise each and every day. Losing twenty pounds in four weeks would be difficult but not impossible. My goal was to eat eight hundred calories a day of protein and certain vegetables while eliminating carbs. That meant no more fried Grouper Po-boys, black beans and rice, Cuban bread, key lime pie or red wine. I might allow myself an occasional Michelob Ultra. I decided to grill my fish, bake the veggies, and drink my limited carbs. For exercise, I would jog the 2.6 miles to Summerland Gym, and for further fitness, I would work out with weights for forty minutes before jogging back home. Before, when I was fit, I could accomplish this in under an hour and a half. Today, I would be lucky to do it in two hours with the obvious reason being my extra weight and lack of energy. In other words, because I am a fat ass! That thought brought a smile.

As I ran up Buccaneer Lane, I turned right onto Cutthroat Drive heading toward Overseas Highway, also known as U.S. 1. In an effort to keep my mind off the agony my body was enduring, I tried to keep my thoughts focused. All I could think about was Dawn and the sleepless nights I had encountered because of some ridiculous disagreement that I don't even remember now. It was hard to believe I had not seen Dawn in more than a month and that we had not talked for six days. Although my heart ached for her, my lungs were gasping for air at the moment. I had reached Overseas Highway and was running east toward Summerland Key. I was in worse shape than I had thought. My shirt and shorts were soaking wet as the poison poured from my pores. After turning south on Key Deer Boulevard, I had less than a mile to go before I reached the ocean and my destination of Summerland Gym. It was a desolate road with no houses or activity. Trying to breathe, I kept running hoping I would not be the twenty-second decimated body the *Key West Times* would write about tomorrow. For the remainder of the run, I tried to make sense of the news and why the bodies had been massacred and butchered. Nothing made sense to me. By the time I finally reached the gym, Lorenzo, my previous trainer, was outside waiting on me.

"You're late. I thought you got lost!" he barked with a huge grin.

"Ha, ha," I replied. "You're lucky I made it at all."

Knowing I had been absent from the gym for a while, he took it fairly easy on me. Lorenzo is from the Philippines and is an excellent trainer. He has the ability to look at someone, warm them up, stretch them, and know exactly what their weaknesses are. Today, he worked my arms and core. Tomorrow, I would feel the pain.

My run back to Cudjoe Key was brutal. The thermometer hit the low nineties, and I thought I was going to hit the pavement. When I finally stumbled into my shower, I had been gone two hours and five minutes. Not impressive but a good start.

From the shower window, I stared out over Cudjoe Bay, and the Atlantic Ocean as cold water covered my tired, hurting, overweight body. Something out on the horizon caught my attention. An interesting and unusual large ship with an obvious red cross on its bow headed south-southeast. Not knowing exactly why, a very disturbing and eerie sensation came over me. At the time, I had no idea my path would soon collide with that of the ship, and the never ceasing nightmares would indeed follow me to my own grave.

Corbett A. Davis Jr.

CHAPTER 16

The star of Ashrafi's two hundred sixty five foot rusty hull plowed through the swelling twelve-foot seas in a hurry. Now only a few miles from Havana, her departure from Key West was abrupt and unscheduled. It was the captain's decision to leave in the secret of darkness, trying not to call attention to their exit. The crew that had screwed up certainly would pay for it later. Allah would demand justice. At the very bottom of the ship, forty feet below the hospital room that housed Dawn's limp body was a holding tank. Originally designed to carry ballast on trips with light cargo, it now was a dark dungeon full of ice and dead bodies. The *Lady Demonia* was not the floating hospital it appeared to be. The Saudi ship was indeed a demon ship just as the locals in Key West had speculated.

The owner of the demonic craft, Muhammad Abdul-Mutaal, was not a Saudi oil magnate at all. His Muslim name means "praised servant of the most high." To help his Muslim people he does not sell oil. He sells body parts from American infidels though the lack of religious beliefs and rejection of Islam has anything to do with his choice of eligible candidates.

His black-market organ donor business originally only had targeted homeless men and women in port cities. These were people no one missed when they disappeared. It did not take Mutaal long to figure out how lucrative international organ trafficking can be. A kidney on the black market sells for a handsome two hundred thousand dollars. A healthy liver could bring even more while the right heart for the right buyer could bring millions. In China, organs are often procured from executed prisoners while in Iran the selling of one's kidneys or other nonlife threatening organs for profit is perfectly legal. In the rest of the world, there is a shortage of organ donors, and often, there is a long list of people waiting to receive a vital organ. And of course, Mutaal is happy that selling one's organs is illegal. It drives up the prices and makes his business much more profitable.

Mutaal's *Star of Ashrafi* was equipped with the latest technology and some of the best doctors and staff in the world. He soon expected his biggest payday since he started the business seven years ago. Aboard the ship at this very moment was a living heart donor with rare Rh-negative blood and a match to the heart needed by the Shah of Iran's very weak and only son. The Shah, one of the wealthiest men in Iran, has offered Mutaal five million dollars for a compatible heart. He awaits word from Mutaal and the ship's captain before he and his son board their private jet to Havana.

With feet and hands still bound, Dawn Landry's five-million-dollar heart beat rapidly as she is tossed about on the table in the twelve-to fifteen-foot rough seas. The only reason the Shaw of Iran is not already in route to Cuba is the same reason the ship left Key West so suddenly.

A week ago, because of a faulty generator, the ice melted in the dark dungeon-like hole that held the organless bodies down below. The stench was unbearable so the crew decided to take the ship out one night into the gulf in order to open the ballast hatch and dump the latest twenty-five bodies. They had no idea a bad storm would hit and scatter the bodies all over the lower Keys. Now the newspaper was reporting twenty-one of the bodies surfaced with missing organs.

Corbett A. Davis Jr.

CHAPTER 17

I still had an unnerving sensation in the pit of my stomach. I wanted to believe it was just soreness from my workout with Lorenzo. "Body by Lo," his bumper stickers boasted. When his clients reach the point where Lorenzo thinks they have worked hard and have made significant fitness progress, his gifts to them included a box of protein shakes, a before and after photo, and one of his famous bumper stickers.

At five feet eight inches, one hundred and forty two pounds, Lorenzo is in great shape. He runs five miles a day, swims two miles, and lifts weights between clients. He told me, "No steroids, no carbs, and no alcohol!" My reply was "Yeah and no fun!" And I had yet to earn a bumper sticker. I knew my arms and chest would ache tomorrow, but the bizarre feeling I now had in my gut remained unexplainable. Somehow, I could not shake the fear I felt. "Fear of what?" I said aloud. Maybe it was Limbo's behavior, or maybe I was anxious to finally see Dawn later today. And could it be possible that there is any connection with that mysterious Red Cross ship I watched earlier from my bathroom window? That's insane, no way! I convinced myself.

Traffic was light, and my ride from Cudjoe Key to Key West took only twenty minutes. When I passed the Waffle House, I was tempted to stop, have a pecan waffle with grits, and talk with Tracy. However, I knew not only was I in a hurry to get to the jewelry store, but also I did not need the carbs or especially the temptation of a beautiful, fit, tan, young, blue-eyed girl who liked to fly-fish. That could mean nothing but trouble. I did stretch my neck as I drove by.

It was still early, and Caribbean Jewelry Company was dark inside. I entered at the rear of the building, turned off the alarm system, and flipped on the lights. My mood immediately brightened up and changed for the better. I felt good here. As I walked through the store, I admired the tasteful décor, the jewelers' benches, and the inventory—reminders of my father everywhere. Charles P. Taylor Sr. had taught me well in the early years. He was a genius in the jewelry trade and the most disciplined man I ever knew. He was respected by everyone he came in contact with. From customers and employees to diamond cutters around the world, he still receives international praise for his work.

I entered through the main door from Duval Street. The design of the store is elegant and sophisticated yet warm and inviting. To the left, the floor cases display all of the finer designer lines and companies. Each one is unique and different and includes big names such as Roberto Coin, David Yurman, Mikimoto, JB Starr, Tacori, A Jaffe, and Scott Kay who are all represented in their own individual setting. To the right, as you walk in, our own original designs of diamond necklaces, earrings, and bracelets fill the first case. Next are our watch lines that include Rolex, Tag Heuer, Tissot, David Yurman, Patek Phillipe, Piaget, and Cartier. Durotrans of beautiful people with beautiful jewelry filled the walls. In the rear of the store are the bookkeeping offices, a diamond room for special showings, and a walk in vault. The diamond room has the same equipment, microscopes, and lighting as the appraisal room in my home. This is also the room where we bring customers when they are looking at expensive loose diamonds or just want privacy when purchasing jewelry for a special someone. The last ruthless owner of Caribbean Jewelers, Winston Sloan, would use this room for very private showings to disgruntled spouses seeking to eliminate their loved ones from the face of the Earth. A large expensive gold sculpture, "The Deadly Reef," as it became known, was a masquerade for the murder that often hatched in this very spot.

This same diamond room is a perfect environment for my work, but I still prefer writing appraisals at my canal side home. It's a more laid-back atmosphere, and there are no interruptions. And my gem lab at home was wired for music. Andrea Bocelli has helped me grade more diamonds than I could possibly count.

At 7:30 a.m., our staff all arrived on time to start the day. Since the summer months in the Keys are considered off-season and tourism is down, we have a limited work force until the winter months arrive. Thomas Erickson, my store manager, is responsible for all hiring and firing. Tom is very good at managing employees and keeps them focused and motivated while continually keeping a close eye on business and customers.

Tom is also a wonderful and understanding friend. Without him over the past few months, business at Caribbean Jewelry Company certainly would have declined. My recently deteriorating lifestyle that has affected my relationship with Dawn could have been disastrous for business. The blame and suffering caused by my shameful neglect of responsibility is solely my fault. Regaining possession and reclamation of my lost values is important but would have to wait until Dawn is safe. And I cannot give one hundred percent until then.

On premises in the jewelry store, we have three full time bench jewelers, four sales girls, two bookkeepers, a hand engraver, and a watchmaker. It's more like a family than a business. Everyone gets along and enjoys the work, Key West, and each other.

Up in Gulf Breeze, there was a time many years back when I worked hard and long, seven days a week, in the jewelry business for my father. I got burned out and moved to the Keys to become a fishing guide and enjoy life. A few years ago, with the help of Limbo, lady luck, and some very peculiar circumstances, I came into a shit load of money. That's when I first learned of Limbo's ties with U.S. Customs and with his unusual source of income. Because of a diabolical woman who became widowed by her own hand, along with her husband's partner, an accomplice named Winston Sloan, Limbo and I split two million dollars. I also inherited Caribbean Jewelry Company formally known as Sloan's Jewelry.

It was Wednesday morning and time for Caribbean Jewelry Company's weekly employee's meeting. Tom Erickson always started and ended the meeting the same way.

"Good morning friends! Remember, if you are in a business and it's not fun, you're in the wrong business."

Every week, after their good-morning greetings, the entire staff enthusiastically recited the quote along with Tom starting the day with positive momentum.

"This morning I want to tell you a funny story about something that happened to me when I was seventeen. I was working in a family-owned jewelry store in Tallahassee while I attended college there. It was early Saturday morning right after we opened the store. The owner was working at his bench and I was on the sales floor. A husband and wife entered the store. They were window shopping, taking their time case by case. She was an attractive woman about fifty years old and was wearing a beautiful bright colored dress, simple diamond earrings, a gold bangle bracelet, a thin serpentine chain around her neck, and a yellow gold engagement ring with about a quarter carat diamond. The man was dressed in ragged blue jeans and a white T-shirt, his hair a mess under his hat. He wore no

Corbett A. Davis Jr.

jewelry except for a plastic Timex watch. His beard was grey, long, and unkempt. I approached the couple with a smile, knowing I was wasting my time, and said, "Good morning, can I help you?"

The lady smiled and replied, "Good morning, yes, we would like to look at some diamonds!"

As Tom spoke, he made eye contact with each and every employee. And as if I were not in the room, he continued.

"The man remained silent. In fact, he looked almost ill. His color was not good, and his cheek was swollen.

I'm sure my eyes were rolling toward the heavens in boredom. Again, realizing I was probably wasting my time, I directed my question to the gentleman in the orange and blue cap with "War Damn Eagle" across the front. "Was there anything particular you were interested in? What shape and size diamond were you thinking about sir?"

Tom stood up, paused for a moment, and watched the expression of each employee as if reading their thoughts to see if they were paying attention. I also looked. They were hanging on every word. Continuing with the story Tom sat back down and said, "The man just stood there staring at me as if he wanted to say something but couldn't. He had a very odd look on his face that I could not read. He turned and walked toward the door to exit. My mind was racing and wondered what the hell was going on. The lady then spoke. I was listening to her but never took my eyes off the man who now was standing on the sidewalk in front of the store.

"We would like to see a big round diamond with some really good colors and none of them black spots in it."

"Sweet Jesus!" I thought aloud.

"Excuse me?" she asked.

"Oh, something around five or six carats maybe?" I said, trying to recover from my surprise at her answer.

Still with one eye on Pa Kettle outside in the street, I began to babble.

"Yes, ma'am, that is a beautiful dress you have on and your husband seems like a very nice man. I think a six-carat diamond would be perfect for your long slender finger. Maybe an E or F color, not flawless but with VVS1 or VVS2 clarity, something that would fit your lifestyle and personality."

The lie left my lips before my brain realized what my words were saying. The lady began speaking, and I did not hear a word she said. I was still fixated on Grizzly Adams outside our store window. The man then walked to the curb, removed his hat, leaned up against someone's brand new Mercedes convertible, opened his mouth, and spit out the most god-awful wad of brown shit-colored chewing tobacco juice. His aim was not good. The slobbery liquid hit the parking meter and splattered all the over the wheel and the man's shoes. He wiped his shoes on the back of each of his pant legs, ran his beard across his shirt sleeve, and reentered our front door.

"Did you hear me, Tom?" the lady said.

I then focused on *ma* as she repeated herself.

"I said I don't know what all them *E*s and *F*s letters and numbers are you were talking about but we want to spend about fifty thousand dollars! You see Mr. Tom, we grow peanuts, and we had a real good year."

By now, I'm thinking either I'm on Candid Camera, or I've just entered Rod Serling's Twilight Zone.

"Yes, ma'am, of course, let me see what we have. I'll be right back!"

I almost ran to the back room. I quickly scanned the sales floor to see if any customers who might have owned the Mercedes had seen Grizzly spit all over it.

Corbett A. Davis Jr.

As I bolted to the back room, I accidently knocked over Mr. Moon, the owner of the store.

"I'm sorry, Mr. Moon," I said, picking him up off the floor.

"What the hell is going on, Tom?" he barked.

"Well, Mr. Moon, I have these two hillbilly redneck peanut farmers out there wasting my time. They say they want to buy a six-carat diamond. The man has chewing tobacco dripping from his beard and the woman acts like Minnie Pearl."

Tom stood again, paused effectively, and said to the employees, "Ya'll listen close now to the lesson I learned that day from Mr. Moon of Moon's Jewelry in Tallahassee." All eyes and ears were alert as Tom remained standing for the close of his story.

Mr. Moon looked at me and said, "Sit down now, Tom! Let me tell you something. You are young and inexperienced or I would fire you right here on the spot. Listen and listen good. That couple might seem to be hillbilly redneck peanut farmers to you, but they are our hillbilly rednecks! Never and I mean never judge people or assume anything from the way a customer looks, dresses, or talks. You understand that, Tom?"

"Yes, sir," I replied as if being scolded by the principal.

"Now, Tom, you go back out there, learn everything you can about them, hold and lightly squeeze her hand. Compliment them on anything you can think of and treat them like you would want to be treated. You are no better than they are and don't ever forget that. In other words, go kiss their ass and take their money."

"Yes, sir," I said, staring at the floor unable to look Mr. Moon in the eye.

"By the time Mr. and Mrs. Robert Dunhill left the store with her new 6.01 ct. round brilliant cut diamond with E color and VVS1 clarity, she knew all about those E and F colors and numbers. That day, I taught them all about diamonds, but they taught me a much more valuable lesson. Although now I am embarrassed about my behavior back then, I never forgot what I learned from Mr. Moon and the Dunhills. Bob and Laverne Dunhill had grown peanuts for thirty years. They retired the day they bought the diamond, which was one week after discovering oil on their North Florida peanut farm. So every time I find myself judging a customer, I think back to that big grin on Mrs. Dunhill's face. She held her diamond up to let the sunlight reflect off of it as they drove off in their Mercedes convertible with that beautiful brown juice dripping off the rear wheel."

All of the employees laughed as Tom finished with his thought of the day.

"One last thing, ladies and gentlemen," Tom said once again with everyone's attention.

"About your competition. Look at their good points and try to improve on them. Look at their bad points and eliminate them."

For a moment, we all were mesmerized. Like a seasoned theologian, Tom moved and motivated us all. That is Tom's strong point. My real contribution comes from years and years of growing up in retail jewelry and having education in gemology, management, and marketing. Between Tom and me, Caribbean Jewelry Company of Key West, Florida, was now one of the most successful stores in the south.

Although I had not been much help at the store lately, my road to recovery would include refocusing on important priorities. And the jewelry store is definitely included in the list of those significant concerns.

As I hurried to Seaman's Hospital, I had mixed emotions. I felt good about my business and the people who worked there, but I felt empty and much anxiety about finally seeing Dawn. Still, somehow I sensed what I was about to discover. And it would not be pleasant.

CHAPTER 18

Running anxiously, I was out of breath when I reached the top of the stairs at Seaman's Hospital. My heart pounded wildly from anticipation, even more so than during a heavy cardio workout.

The nurse's station on the fifth floor seemed hectic and chaotic. Nurses were running around nervously, doctors looked panicked, and numerous monitors' screens beeped with no audience. Patients seemed annoyed and distant.

I was finally able to get the attention of an intern.

"What's going on?" I asked.

"No time to explain right now!" he barked back.

Everyone on the whole floor acted as if they were expecting an earthquake. Chaos was obvious. I grabbed a nurse by the arm as she tried to run by ignoring me.

"Where is Dawn Landry's room?" I asked.

She pulled from me and ran away crying.

"What the hell is going on here lady?" I screamed in her direction.

She stopped, turned, and looked at me. Her eyes were swollen and filled with tears.

"Are you a relative of hers?" she asked.

"Yes! I'm her husband," I lied back.

"Come here," she said as she grabbed me and pushed me into a small utility closet.

I noticed her nametag, and as calmly as possible, I asked again, "What the hell is going on here Miss Garcia?"

Through the window of the closed door, I saw police officers arrive, and the Coast Guard walk by.

"Something bad happened here, is that right?"

"Yes, you're right, Mr. Landry," she replied.

"Taylor, my name is Powell Taylor," I said, not thinking.

"I thought you said you and Dawn were married?" Nurse Garcia asked with a surprised look on her face.

"Uh, yeah that's right, but she goes by her maiden name," I muttered, trying to cover my fib.

"What happened here?" I continued.

As she spoke, it was as if I was in a vacuum. All I could hear was her voice. It was as if no one else existed on the floor. Everyone moved in slow motion, and oddly, there was no background noise or voices.

"There are people missing, Mr. Taylor. Four patients, an intern, and two new nurses have disappeared."

My heart skipped a beat and then began pounding loud enough to be heard without a stethoscope. I didn't need to ask, but I did anyway.

"Is Dawn one of the missing?"

When she nodded, it was like someone pressed the mute button back on. Loud noises, voices, and confusion returned immediately as if on cue.

"Dr. Shezad, is that the intern that is missing?" I asked.

"How did you know that?" Nurse Garcia asked with a confused stare.

Nurse Garcia handed me her business card and said call her anytime. She then ran down the corridor with tears still flowing. Trying to remain as calm as possible and not panic, I dialed Limbo's cell number.

Corbett A. Davis Jr.

Relieved that he actually answered, I shouted out, "Limbo, I need your help! I need it now! Meet me at Jose's Cantina on White Street in twenty minutes."

Jose's was the only place close to the hospital I could think of.

CHAPTER 19

When Limbo walked through the front door of the restaurant he looked as if I interrupted his swim. His hair was wet, and he wore white linen pants, a long-sleeved aqua color linen shirt, his signature long billed cap, and flip-flops. Limbo's eyes told me he recognized the concern and my need for a friend when he arrived.

Although Jose's Cantina is not on Duval Street where most of the tourists swarm, the restaurant was packed today. By the time Limbo and I met there, it was busy with the local lunch crowd. We sat in the back of the café at a table for two set with plastic tablecloths, red linen napkins, and stainless steel silverware. Each table had a fresh cut flower, salt, pepper, and a bottle of Rickey's Hot Sauce. Black and white photos of a time gone by in Cuba hung proudly on every wall. Latin music filled the air while customers chatted loudly in Spanish. The floors and counters were spotlessly clean and the only smells present were those of aromatic Cuban food cooking in the kitchen.

I ordered a bowl of black beans and rice and a cup of café con leche. Limbo decided on a Cuban sandwich with a Cuban beer. I still was not used to seeing Limbo back to drinking alcohol. My concern must have been obvious. Limbo said, "It's okay, Powell, I've got it under control."

I wondered just what he had under control; his drinking, his dark thoughts, his health or his life. I just nodded and ignored the comment.

I began at the very beginning trying to paint a complete picture for Limbo so he could better understand the danger involved with Dawn's disappearance.

"Limbo, I am very worried that something bad has happened or is about to happen to Dawn." I started, "As you know, we had a stupid fight quite a few weeks ago, and I haven't talked with her since. She had left messages on my cell phone, but they all stopped seven days ago."

"Tell me everything that has happened in the past month, Powell, anything you can think of that may or may not have to do with Dawn or her disappearance," Limbo said.

I told him about all the conversations I had with Dr. Shezad and the nurses at Seaman's Hospital. He was curious that I was never allowed to speak with her. I told him that no one was helpful and that they just pissed me off with their unconcerned attitude each time I spoke with them. I finished by telling him what nurse Garcia had told me that Dr. Shezad, four patients, and two nurses are all missing. And of course, one of these patients was Dawn. I added, "Dawn, the love of my life that I abandoned over some meaningless quarrel. And now, I may never see her again!"

"Calm down, think positive, Powell. We'll figure this out and find her," Limbo said unconvincingly.

"Did this nurse Garcia seem genuine and concerned? Do you think she was being honest Powell?" Limbo continued.

"Yes, definitely. She was sobbing, crying through the whole ordeal of speaking with me. She even gave me her cell phone number and told me to call her anytime."

Just as Limbo was saying we needed to speak with her as soon as possible and get some information, I heard someone enter the restaurant.

"Mr. Taylor!" A familiar voice called out.

I turned and to my surprise there stood Nurse Garcia still dressed in her white uniform.

"I hope you don't mind me tracking you down like this. I heard you earlier on your cell phone at the hospital asking someone to meet you here."

Nurse Garcia looked to be in her midforties, with dark brown eyes that matched the color of her hair. Her huge bright smile seemed a perfect complement. The dark skin, heavy accent, and last name convinced me she was of Cuban descent. Her thirty or more extra pounds probably came from a hectic work schedule that permitted no exercise. And the black beans, yellow rice, and fried pork chunks weren't exactly diet food.

"Please join us, Nurse Garcia," I said as I pulled up a chair from another table.

"Consuella, please call me Consuella," Nurse Garcia said as she sat down.

Limbo finally spoke, "Consuella, my name is Dr. James Adams and we were just about to call you. Thank you for coming, and we do need your help desperately. But tell me, why did you come?"

When Limbo spoke as Dr. Adams, the calming tone of his voice exuded credibility. He gave the correct impression that he could be trusted and was genuinely concerned.

"Over the last couple of weeks, Dawn and I became fairly close. She told me all about Powell and their quarrel. She also said it was minor, and she loved him and could not wait to get out of the hospital and make up for the lost time."

Although it was exactly what I wanted to hear, it did not ease my pain at all. Consuella Garcia continued to tell us about all of the concerns she had reported to her supervisor lately. New interns and staff were not professional, helpful, or qualified. And one of the reasons she followed me today was that Dawn was also concerned and scared. She had been admitted for anemia and head trauma but was feeling fine three days before they all disappeared. Dawn had told her about my phone messages that said they would not let me visit because she was too weak and still in ICU. The lies and insensitivity along with keeping her against her will frightened the hell out of her. I was feeling sick to my stomach and could not eat my lunch.

"Consuella, could you tell us anything you can about the intern, Dr. Shezad, I believe is his name, or any of the staff that left abruptly? Anything and everything even if it sounds unimportant," Limbo asked.

"I really can't tell you much except that they were all loners that hung out together. They never talked with the regular staff. They ate lunch together, worked the same shifts together, and drove to and from work together. I never could get straight answers from any of the supervisors. It's almost as if they all just showed up one day."

"Okay, Consuella, did you ever know where they were from or who hired them?" I interrupted.

"No! Never. But wait, I almost forgot. I did see Dr. Shezad in Key West one day. It was my day off, and I had taken my daughter to lunch down on the harbor. I remember being very surprised to see him getting off the big ship."

"A cruise ship?" Limbo asked.

My thoughts began to race as I broke out in a cold sweat. Somehow, knowing what Nurse Garcia was about to say I listened in silence and sadness.

"Not a cruise ship at all. It was that big medical research vessel that was anchored in the harbor for a week or so!"

"The one with the big red crosses on the bow?" I snapped, already knowing her answer.

"Yes! That's the one. I never did believe that Shezad was capable of doing medical charity work or having any compassion at all. That is why I was so surprised to see him leaving the ship. When I saw him at work the next day, he was very shady about it. Out of curiosity, I asked him what he was doing there. He told me I had made a mistake. It wasn't him, and he never went to any ship. I knew he was lying but figured he was just being his usual asshole self. Oh, sorry!" she finished.

Limbo and I caught each other's eye while the three of us sat in silence for a few minutes.

"Are you going to eat those beans and rice, Mr. Taylor?" Consuella asked.

"No! Not hungry."

"You mind?" she said as she grabbed my spoon.

"I tend to eat when I'm nervous and upset. Actually, I tend to eat when I'm happy and not upset. I just love to eat," she said, trying to change the mood, I suspect.

We all forced a smile.

"Let me ask you something, Nurse Garcia," Limbo began.

"Consuella, please, it's Consuella," she interrupted.

"Okay, Consuella, let me ask you. Have you read about any of these desecrated bodies that are showing up in our waters? Have they brought any of these bodies to the hospital that you know of?" Limbo asked.

"Oh sweet Jesus! You don't think that these are related to our missing patients, do you?" she cried.

Limbo and I did not answer her. We remained silent, waiting until she continued.

"Actually, they did bring a few in for autopsies. It was quite disturbing, as you can imagine. The first two bodies they found we mistakenly reported to the *Key West Times*. From the condition of the disfigured bodies, they wrongly reported it as possible shark attacks. Later, from dental records, the police identified the couple as newlyweds from Ponchatoula, Louisiana, who had come to Key West for their honeymoon. The second night here they ate conch salad from a street-side vendor down in Bahamas Town. They both became very ill with food poisoning. That's the problem with conch salad. It's made with raw conch meat and marinated in lime and orange juices with onions, peppers, and a little vinegar. The problem is that it's illegal to harvest conch in Florida. All of the conch meat comes from the Bahamas, and buying it from a street-side vendor is dangerous. If it's old or sits out in the sun, it will do a number on your digestive system.

"Even in their bloated stage of decomposition, I immediately recognized the couple they brought in. They had spent a day on my floor recuperating from the food poisoning. I had assumed they got better and checked out. But I found out later from the police that no one saw them after they were admitted to the hospital."

Nurse Garcia stopped for a moment as if trying to recall any more information. With a puzzled look on his face, Limbo spoke.

"What do you remember about the bodies and the autopsy?"

Consuella Garcia snapped out of her concentration and answered, "It was very disturbing to say the least. We assumed from the newspaper report that it was a shark attack, but I had my doubts. After the autopsy was performed, I spoke with the pathologist, and he confirmed my fears."

"Their eyes were missing but with no signs of metabolic breakdown around the sockets. In other words, no microorganisms or sea life such as crabs, sharks, or any other scavengers caused the missing eyeballs. And even though the bodies were past fresh decomposition and in a bloated stage, their abdomens were not overall bloated from the normal accumulation of gases such as hydrogen sulfide, carbon dioxide, or methane."

Limbo interrupted, "If the body was not bloated from gases, why did you consider it to be in the bloated stage of decomposition, and how can a body be considered bloated when no gases are present?"

"Very good question," she replied. "The easiest way to answer that, Dr. Adams, is like this. The bodies had not yet started to actively decay but had been in the water long enough to no longer be considered in the fresh stage of decomposition. There were no gases present in either body cavity; thus, the result was no distention of the abdomen. The reason for the lack of body fluids, liquids, and gases was not only very frightening but also obvious. The couple had been cut and their stomachs filleted methodically with both hearts and kidneys missing. It was a very precise surgical procedure."

"Holy hell!" I said in disbelief. "You mean someone is illegally harvesting body parts the way some old Key Westers illegally poach lobster?"

"It's much worse than you think, Powell," she continued.

"I'm not sure how many bodies they have found so far, but I know it's more than twenty. And all of them were missing vital organs. To the dismay of the Chamber of Commerce, the *Key West Times* keeps reporting and assuming that we have a bizarre bull shark problem in the lower Keys. So far, the hospital has not told them anything to the contrary."

"Twenty-one bodies," Limbo whispered.

"And wait until the Lower Keys Chamber of Commerce finds out the truth. They're going to wish we had bull sharks gone mad."

The restaurant was cleared out, and we were the only table remaining. It was almost three in the afternoon, and it was too early for the dinner crowd and too late for lunch. After listening to Nurse Garcia for over two and a half hours, Limbo and I thanked her for her time and told her we would not rest or give up until all questions were answered. I wrote down her phone number and assured her that I would call her when we learned the truth of the murders and the whereabouts of Dawn. Leaving Jose's Cantina, Consuella tried to force a genuine smile while saying, "I know you'll find her safe, Powell. Good luck!"

As much as I wanted to believe her, I knew it was very likely that Dawn would never be safe again.

"I've got work to do Powell, let's go!" Limbo snapped.

CHAPTER 20

Before Limbo met me at my house he needed to stop at his place and pick up some charts of the local waters while I went to the 7-Eleven on Big Coppitt Key and bought two six packs of Hatuey. I knew the Cuban beer would help us get through the evening.

We arrived at my house on Cudjoe Key about the same time. Limbo with his charts and me with the beer, we sat on the back deck to discuss and plan our next move.

"This doesn't look good, Powell." Limbo started.

I opened two beers, handed one to Limbo, sat down, and answered him.

"I know, and I am worried about Dawn. Do you think we are too late?"

"No, not at all, Powell. We have to think positive. But we have no time to waste. I have to be honest with you. Time is running out."

I knew he was right but did not want to admit it. She had to be okay. I never said good-bye. I never told her how sorry I was about our fight. I needed to explain things, tell her I love her and miss her, and can't live without her. I wondered where she was at this moment. Is she safe? Is she in pain? Is Dawn even alive?

"Limbo, we need to do something. We can't just sit here. We have to find Dawn. Where do we start?" I asked.

"Well, Powell," Limbo said, "what do we have so far? You have not been able to reach Dawn for weeks now. She was last seen at the hospital and disappeared with the others."

"Yes!" I interrupted. "And she is missing along with that Dr. Shezad. I knew there was a reason I didn't like him when we spoke."

I could tell Limbo's brain was racing. He finally spoke.

"Yeah, Powell, and things are beginning to fall into place. Nurse Garcia saw Dr. Shezad coming off that Red Cross ship in Key West. That ship disappeared about the same time as he, Dawn, and the others did. Twenty-one bodies have been found floating from Sawyer Key to Key West. The last body was found two days ago."

"That's the same day I saw from my bathroom window that ship sailing south," I added.

"It's beginning to make sense, Powell."

"It is?" I said.

"Here's what I believe is happening. Dr. Shezad is obviously associated with the medical ship that was anchored in Key West. Nurse Garcia proved that. What if that ship is not a floating charity hospital like they claim? What if it is a vessel that houses physicians and nurses that harvest organs and sell them to the highest bidders?"

"As much as I hope you are wrong, it does make sense, Limbo! Where do you think the ship is headed? Do you think Dawn is aboard?" I asked, not really wanting an honest answer. I knew the chances were likely that Dawn's body could wash up next.

"I think they are headed to Cuba or maybe the Dominican Republic," Limbo answered.

"Well, let's go!" I yelled.

"We will, Powell, but first, I want to calculate the tides and currents for the past two days since the last body was found."

CHAPTER 21

"Limbo, are you sure your calculations are accurate?" I asked as our skiff slammed into the waves across Boca Grande Channel on a southwest heading to the Marquesas.

"Hell yeah, I'm sure!" he barked back.

"I've been studying these waters since before you were born."

"I know, Limbo," I said. "But I thought maybe you might have been smokin' a little rope that night and you could be off a few degrees or more."

"Look, just keep the fucking skiff on a 220 degree course; I take this shit seriously," Limbo said as he pointed to the compass.

The wind was blowing hard today from the southeast with a swift falling tide. This made Boca Grande Channel more treacherous than ever to cross. The current and wind were competing against each other and the five-foot seas were confused and agitated and reacting with mostly white water. Occasionally, a rogue wave would break over the bow and drench Limbo and me.

"Keep going." He would cry out.

I'm sure he said it just to aggravate me. He knew there was no way I would give up our quest for answers or more importantly our search for Dawn. I hoped and prayed that our instincts were wrong. When we finally came out of the tumultuous waters of the channel, we hit a calm surface that lowered the bow so I was able to speed up. My brain was on autopilot and my concern for Dawn was discouraging and bleak.

How could this be? What possibly could be the reason for Dawn's disappearance? Although the skies cleared and the Atlantic's surface calmed down, an ill feeling came over me. A knot in the pit of my stomach would not ease. Bad karma seemed to follow our wake like sea gulls behind a shrimp boat. And I could not shake the image of a red cross on the bow of a passing ship.

I was so deep in a trance that I did not hear Limbo's scream. Pointing dead ahead, he shook me hard. It was like coming out of a deep sleep. I jumped up as my eyes followed the direction of Limbo's pointing finger to a small isle of mangrove trees. The sky was bright blue and cloudless as I turned the bow of the skiff toward the deserted mangrove island. When we got closer, Limbo said, "Look, Powell! What is that in the sky above the trees?"

I squinted and looked hard. Even with my polarized glasses, I could not make out what caused the shadow in the air.

"Holy shit!" Limbo yelled. "It's fucking vultures, thousands of them."

What a dreadful sight and an even worse realization. I felt ill again. My stomach cramped and my thoughts were garbled. I broke out in a cold sweat. Realizing what was about to happen, I jerked the throttle back bringing the skiff to a sudden stop.

"What the hell?" Limbo yelled as he was almost thrown overboard off the bow. When he turned back to look me in the eye, I was doubled over the gunnel, puking my breakfast into the clean waters of the Atlantic Ocean.

When I recovered, I washed my face with seawater and sat down.

"What do you think, Limbo?" I asked cautiously, knowing what his answer would be.

"Powell, we are thirty-five miles from the closest land. This is not good. I remember studying the behavior of vultures years ago when I was investigating some random murders in the Everglades."

"With Customs?" I asked, hoping to get a little more info on his personal life.

"Yeah, Powell, that's right. You asked me a question, so do you want an answer or not?" he snapped.

"Not if you're gonna be a dick about it!" I snapped.

"Okay, okay, I'm sorry, Powell. Here's what I know about vultures. There are two types of vultures that live in South Florida, the black vultures and the turkey vultures. See that one right there, Powell?" Limbo said as he pointed to one with a red head sitting in the mangroves.

I nodded, and he continued.

"That's a turkey vulture, named from his bald redhead that resembles a wild turkey. Their wingspan can reach six feet. The reason they have a bald head is because vultures are scavengers that feed on dead animals. They often stick their heads inside the body cavity of the rotting animals. If the head had feathers and was not bald, it would catch pieces of decayed meat causing bacteria and harmful microorganisms to grow. They have a great sense of smell and possibly found whatever dead animals they are feeding on only twenty-four hours after they died."

"Even this far offshore?" I interrupted.

"Yes, Powell, they also have a very sharp eye. And although the vulture is a very gentle and nonaggressive bird, he is pretty damn disgusting. Whenever the buzzard feels threatened by a predator moving in on his find, it vomits semidigested food. The foul smell of that food forces the predators to move away from it. And the body weight of the bird gets reduced, allowing it to fly away quickly."

Corbett A. Davis Jr.

"Shit, Limbo, eating and walking around in dead bodies can't be healthy, not even for a buzzard. How come they don't catch some disease?" I said.

"These birds were made to live and dine on dead shit. They are like machines built to deal with such a foul environment. Vultures survive because of some very peculiar habits. They urinate on their own legs to cool themselves in the hot summer months. The strong acid of the urine also kills the bacteria when the bird walks on decaying animal bodies.

"I'm sure you've seen buzzards sitting in the tops of trees with their wings spread out. Not only does this warm their bodies in cooler months and dry their wings, it also destroys bacteria by baking them in the sun."

"Wow, who taught 'em that, Limbo?" I said with a grin.

Limbo looked like he was going to say something but then just shook his head as if he were irritated, so I quickly said, "Thanks, Limbo, I really feel much better now." I quipped sarcastically. I punched the throttle forward, and we eased toward the island. As we approached, the birds ignored us. They continued to circle above, blocking the sun, and casting a shadow over the entire island. Others dove down. Some rode the erratic wind currents while others perched themselves in the top of the mangrove trees.

The wind had stopped and the heat was unbearable, and when I slowed the boat, the foul scent of low tide filled the air, striking my senses as if I were a blind man relying only on my sense of smell. But the closer we got to the mangroves, the more the odor reeked of rot. It was not just decaying sargasso weed uncovered by the low water. And before I could say anything, Limbo beat me to it.

"What the fuck is that smell?" he said.

We both knew exactly what it was, rotting flesh. We circled the island hoping to find a decayed rotting whale or dolphin afloat. But predictably, that was not what we found. The first body we saw was an upper torso with no head or arms. All the blood left my head; I felt weak and faint.

"Lie down fast and put your legs in the air!" Limbo yelled.

When I did, I felt the blood rush back to my face.

"You okay, Powell?"

"No, I'm not, Limbo. Look at that," I said, pointing to the remains. "It's a woman's body!" Although the vultures had plucked hard at the flesh, one breast implant still hung by a thread.

I slowly maneuvered the skiff and asked Limbo to grab the implant. He did not question the reason as I was certain he knew why. Barely visible, stamped on the base of the silicone breast was not only an identification number and the manufacturer's name but also a size, DOW #SZ236INT 34DD. When Limbo read the number aloud, I was sick again. With nothing left in my stomach, I cramped up over the gunnel as my body spasmed and twisted in pain. I thought of a much happier time when Dawn and I were drinking and laughing on Cudjoe Key one night. It had been two years since she told me the story of when she got her breast implants. It brought smiles to us both when she asked, "Are they too big for you Powell, these fabulous size 34 double Ds?" There was no smile on my face now.

Limbo radioed Customs giving them our GPS coordinates and explained the grim situation.

Something caught my attention in a nearby Mangrove root. With no concern at all of our presence, the buzzard's red wrinkled face looked like an old woman who had spent most of her life in the sun. There was sadness deep in the bird's piercing eyes. Or maybe it was determination. Either way, it surely was an occupational hazard that came from preying on the sick and dying. These buzzards were not much different than the human vultures that provided this meal.

Corbett A. Davis Jr.

We had been idling in awkward silence for quite some time. Limbo glanced back at me as if he were going to say something. He never did. To break the silence, I said, "Hey, Limbo, I've never seen the tide so low. It's extremely low, right?"

"Yeah, Powell," Limbo answered, "It is very low, in fact it's dead low!"

Limbo turned and continued staring northward over the bow. I wondered what deep hole his mind had slipped into this time.

We did not wait for Customs or the Coast Guard to arrive. We were in Boca Grande Channel headed back to Key West when we saw the first helicopter fly over. Limbo would find out later that four more bodies were found on this day.

CHAPTER 22

Forgetting to lock my front door was a bad habit I needed to work on.

"It's not her, Powell," Limbo barked from the foot of my bed.

"What?" I managed to say, still half asleep, and startled by his presence.

I looked over at the clock next to my bed to see what time it was. The clock's neon digits were flashing rapidly. The power must have gone off while I was out. I tried to focus on my watch. It was a little after 3:00 a.m.

Although slightly disorientated, it suddenly hit me. It wasn't Dawn's body we found floating south of the Marquesas.

"Who was it, Limbo?" I shouted back.

"Well, according to the report U.S. Customs just faxed over, her name was Sarah Hinson. She was twenty-six years old, graduated from University of Florida in Gainesville and lived in Tampa for the past two years. Here, you read it," Limbo said, handing me the fax.

I scanned the letter quickly. The photo of Sarah reminded me of Dawn, a blonde, blue-eyed beauty with a great smile. It saddened me as I read further. Sarah had been missing for more than three weeks now. Her parents said she had been playing volleyball on the beach in Tampa with friends when she broke her arm. The last person who saw her alive was one of those friends that drove her to the emergency room.

I paused trying to make some sense of it all and asked Limbo, "Does that make sense to you?"

"Yes, it does, Powell. Unfortunately, it does!" he replied.

"The *Mercy Ship*, as the *Tampa Tribune* called it, was anchored in Tampa's harbor for three days before heading to Key West."

"I guess we are on the right tract after all," I said. "What now?" I added.

"For starters, Powell, start locking your front door," Limbo said.

"Don't worry about it. What's next?"

Limbo grabbed my phone and said, "While I call my friend Bob in Washington, you get your skiff ready for a ride across the gulf."

"Where are we headed?" I asked. "And who's Bob?"

"Cuba, and Bob is who will get us clearance to the communist island."

Then I made the mistake of asking, "Is Bob some big shot? How can he get us into Cuba?"

Dr. Adams answered, "Yeah, he's a big shot, Powell. He's Adm. Robert Papp, the commandant of the Coast Guard. He's the only four-star admiral in the Coast Guard, was appointed by the president of the United States, and reports directly to Homeland Security."

"Wow, I guess it's not what you know, it's who you know, right?" I said sarcastically.

"Yeah, Powell, that's right, but who you know is usually because of what you know. Besides, he's a good friend."

Well, Limbo, if Bob is what you say he is and such a good friend, why can't he just send the Coast Guard and Customs to Cuba? Their agents would easily and quickly intercept the evil Saudi ship. Boarding and searching the vessel would surely be easier for them than for us. Besides, isn't it their job?"

"Powell, I have already looked into that and got nowhere. I didn't tell you about the conversation because it was disappointing and tenebrific."

"What, Limbo? Ten of what?"

I was reading concern on Limbo's face when he answered as Dr. Adams.

"Tenebrific, Powell. Depressing and bleak. I've not only contacted Customs and the Coast Guard, but I also talked with the Department of Homeland Security in Washington. Without more evidence, they are not interested in stopping a ship from Saudi Arabia while in Cuban waters, especially a floating charity hospital."

Still not understanding, I asked, "What about the dead bodies floating across the lower Keys? Is that not enough evidence? Did that not get their attention?"

"Yes, Powell, it did, but you do not want to know their answer."

"Try me," I blurted out.

"Okay," he said. "They are convinced that even if what we say is true, by the time they board the vessel in Cuba, it will be too late. They believe no one, this is no American, will be found. In other words, all of the bodies will already have been discarded overboard."

Limbo was right. The idea of Dawn's carved up body floating abandoned in the gulf waters was bleak.

Next Limbo explained just how his admiral friend would help us.

"Since President Kennedy placed an embargo on Cuba in 1962, the Coast Guard has enforced the unauthorized entry into Cuban waters. And in 2003 and 2004, the Bush administration directed the Department of Homeland Security to strengthen enforcement of the embargo by increasing inspections and targeting illegal travel."

I had heard enough. I stopped Limbo from continuing.

Corbett A. Davis Jr.

"I get it. I get it, Limbo. That's why we need your big-shot admiral friend."

I knew now that we would be alone on this trip. No help, no backup, and no records if something went wrong.

I left it at that, feeling certain we would have no problem getting into Cuba.

"Oh! Limbo, what all should I load onto the skiff?"

"Anything and everything you think we'll need to cross the gulf and return. It's a five- or six-hour run one way depending on weather, so bring some drinks and snacks," Limbo said. "But no bananas! We need all the luck we can get," he added.

I had heard plenty of stories why bananas were bad luck on the boat, but I had to hear Limbo's version. So I asked, "Why no bananas, Limbo? And where did this bullshit superstition start?"

"It's not bullshit, Powell, and you know it. Bananas on the boat are disastrous. I've always heard it started back in the days of Captain Hook and sailing ships that traveled the oceans for months at a time. However, it wasn't pirates, storms, or shipwrecks that took most of the lives of the crews. It was disease, the worst of them being scurvy. The old sea captains would try to get as much citrus and fruits at each port that they could gather in order to prevent scurvy. The fruit was kept in large covered bins below the deck to help keep them from ripening too quickly. If a banana was put in the bin by mistake, it put off a gas that sped up the ripening process of the citrus. That was the first sign that bananas were bad luck on a boat. So yeah, Powell after hundreds of years, I'm still superstitious. Leave the fucking bananas at home."

CHAPTER 23

When Dawn would periodically drift back into consciousness, she learned to lie still and listen first. With her eyes closed, she would concentrate on seeing what she heard. This time was different. She heard only the vibration of the engines plowing through the seas. It was a different sound than normal, with a much lower throbbing. She finally grasped the idea of what was different. She envisioned the boat at a slower speed, maneuvering through a smaller waterway. Fear suddenly came over her as she thought to herself, "Is this the end, the final destination?"

Dawn slowly opened one eye then the other. For the first time since her nightmare had begun, there was no one in the room with her. She looked down realizing she was still very cold and still very naked. The sheet that once covered her nude body was now on the floor. Dawn's memory returned in an instant. Dr. Shezad had removed the covering when secretly exploring Dawn's body not so long ago. The sexual touching had aroused and stimulated the perverted intern. But then, remembering the sound of his neck snapping like a chicken bone, the chill of fright set in. Dawn was suddenly determined to fight back and knew she had to escape from her present prison. She raised her head and looked around the room. To her surprise, her left hand pulled free.

Nothing made sense to her, but the nylon tie that had held her wrist so tightly had been cut. She thought Dr. Shezad must have cut it during his last visit while assuming he would rape her lifeless body.

Dawn was able to roll over on her right side from her waist up. Her right arm and both legs were still tightly bound. She pulled at the nylon tie on her right arm. It would not give at all. She looked over both sides of her hospital style bed and down to the floor. Something shiny caught her eye. Stretching out as far as her limber body would allow she noticed it was a surgeon's scalpel. Although very sloppy behavior for her enemies, it would do her no good at all. The knife was unreachable. Frustrated, Dawn fell back, pounding the side of her bed with her free hand. Over and over, she beat the bed, writhing from the waist down as tears filled her eyes once again. "Why me?" She kept thinking. It was no use. She could not get free. The more she twisted, squirmed, and struggled, the more frustrated she became. She wanted to scream as loud as she could out of pure terror but somehow found the ability to remain silent. Dawn did not want anyone to return to the room.

Abruptly and unexpectedly, an intense pain in Dawn's hand caught her attention. Blood covered her fingers and the bed sheets. As she searched for the cause of the gash while feeling under the edge of the bedside, the ship slammed its engine into reverse. If not tied down, Dawn would have been slung off the Gurney feet first. That only told her that her feet faced toward the bow of the boat. She hoped that information might be useful later though she seriously doubted it at this moment.

A loose bolt with a sharp edge had cut Dawn's pinky and ring finger deeply. Focused and determined, she stretched down, barely able to reach the head of the bolt and began to unscrew it. She knew if the ship had stopped, it was possible someone would be coming for her soon. Dawn continued working on the screw, but it was taking forever. Finally, the bolt was free in her left hand. It was a large, thick stainless steel bolt about seven inches long. She immediately sat up and began cutting away at the strap on her right hand. Using the threads like a serrated saw blade, she sawed back and forth until finally, snap! Both hands were free. She was then able to hang over the side of the bed, held only by her feet and grab the scalpel. She easily cut both straps on her feet, and for the first time in four weeks, she was free. She had to get off of this ship, end this horrific nightmare, and find Powell soon. The goose bumps from the cold sterile room reminded her she was still naked. All she found in the cabinet were her panties. She assumed the perverted doctor kept them for a trophy. She slipped them on and was surprised to find the door unlocked.

Corbett A. Davis Jr.

CHAPTER 24

I spent all day in preparation for our early morning departure to Cuba. The skiff was loaded with everything Limbo and I had anticipated we would need on the trip. We both had made lists and notes and checked them numerous times. I had plenty of drinking water, food, snacks, ice, extra fuel, life raft, EPIRB, two satellite phones, two VHF radios, and two handheld GPSs as backup in case we lost power or had problems with the main GPS mounted on the console of the skiff. We also brought two rods and reels to troll through the Gulf Stream. The idea was to catch a few dolphin to present to the first Cubans we would encounter at the marina. Also packed were plenty of ropes, dock lines, and all of the clothes we would need.

Since I do not believe in superstitions, in the bottom of the tackle box, I hid two bananas. My plan was to pull them out for a toast as soon as we safely arrived at Marina Hemingway in Havana. This obviously would convince Limbo how absurd his irrational notion that bananas are bad luck really is. They should bring a smile I thought.

Limbo was just as busy today preparing as I was. He had spent many hours doing the necessary homework that this trip demanded. Figuring fuel consumption and chartering a course with estimated times in an assortment of numerous sea conditions are not an easy task, at least not for me. After receiving the paperwork from Limbo's friend at the Coast Guard, we added to the pile our passports, a quarantine flag, a Cuban flag, and all of the other necessary documents that were required to enter a communist country. But the most impressive bit of preparation by Limbo was a well-hidden false floor under the starboard rear hatch. Earlier, I had watched as Limbo stored two large knives with leather scabbards, a pair of pistols, and a sawed off twelve-gauge shotgun beneath the floor under the boat's batteries and bilge pumps. Limbo gave me a quick lesson on the use of the Glock 9mm and the Sig Sauer 1911 semiautomatic. I already knew how to use the other three weapons.

In the earlier fax from Limbo's friend, Admiral Papp gave us the exact coordinates for the location of the *Star of Ashrafi*. The "ghost ship" had just arrived at longitude 82 degrees 29' 48.08" W and latitude 23 degrees 5' 20.28" N, nine miles west of Havana at Marina Hemingway.

By sunset, we were completely prepared for our one hundred mile trip across the Gulf of Mexico. My Maverick skiff, fully loaded, hung in the boathouse rigged, and ready as if she were going into battle. And unfortunately, that seemed a strong possibility.

Limbo left early to get a good night's rest. He told me to get some sleep, and he would be back at 5:00 a.m. I was starving and decided that I better get a good meal in order to function at one hundred percent tomorrow. Not one of my better decisions.

I did not want to get caught up in conversation or answering questions tonight. So it was easy not to go to Coco's Cantina for dinner. I love Carlos and Flora, but it would turn into a late evening. Within walking distance of my home is one of the best restaurants in all of the Florida Keys. In a big square block building, nothing fancy on the outside, the Square Grouper restaurant was packed with customers when I arrived.

Inside the Grouper, you will always find the perfect mix of chatter, restaurant sounds, and fun. And tonight would prove to be more fun than I ever could have imagined. My plan was to eat light, have a couple beers, and get a good night's rest. Five o'clock would come soon enough. After I ordered my two favorite tapas specials of fried conch with ponzu and wasabi drizzle and the fried eggplant stack with pesto, goat cheese, and marinara, I remembered thinking, "so much for eating light." Reading the specials on the wine menu, I decided to pass on the Corona Light and ordered a 2005 bottle of Jarvis Cabernet instead. It seemed much more aristocratic and appropriate than a beer. I embarrassingly laughed aloud, drawing a little too much attention to my table where I sat alone. Sipping my first glass, I noticed that the crowd was especially lively tonight.

A rather plain, boring looking building on the outside, you would never know you are on Cudjoe Key twenty-two miles east of Key West. You would more likely think you were inside a popular New York hot spot. This happy environment felt good. For a moment, my mind was in a different place where my troubles and the concern for Dawn did not exist.

The table next to mine was especially boisterous and festive. When I turned their way, I noticed that all six were sharing the Square Grouper magical brownie dessert. One of the six noticed my stare, held up a fork of brownie and ice cream while chocolate sauce dripped from her lips, and said, "Cheers!" I held up my wine glass and answered, "Chin-chin!" A smile came across my face as the clinking of forks continued, echoing throughout the whole restaurant. When my dinner arrived, I was on my third glass of Jarvis. Consumed with the creative presentation of the conch dish, I was startled when someone sat down across from me.

"Mind if I join you, Powell?" a lovely voice asked.

"Oh! Uh, no of course not." I managed to answer before following with, "What in the world are you doing here?"

Her eyes were much bluer than I had remembered. Her hair was shoulder length and lighter in color. With very tanned bronze skin, her smile told me she was glad to see me again. Looking more rested and fresh than the first time I had met her in Waffle House, Tracy asked me, "Do you remember me?"

"Of course I do. The gorgeous, blue-eyed brunette from Mobile, Alabama that works at Waffle House in Key West and loves to fly-fish." I spit out.

Then I noticed her T-shirt with the familiar Square Grouper Bar and Grill logo saying "My Favorite Joint."

"I work here now, Powell. In fact, I just got off. Mind if I join you?"

"Not at all, please do," I replied.

There is an unusual innocence and sensuality in Tracy's beauty that is mesmerizing. And at this very minute, it scared the hell out of me. When we met before, I was able to resist Tracy's invitation to fish. Dawn was on my mind, as she still was. But tonight, temptation would be much more difficult to abstain from. Using no common sense whatsoever, as Tracy ordered the yellowtail snapper special, I added yet another bottle of Jarvis Cab. For what seemed to be hours, we drank, laughed, and enjoyed each other's company. It was a reprieve I desperately needed.

Finally, Lynn, the owner, came by our table and asked, "Would you like to spend the night? I'm going home, but I can leave you the key."

Looking around the restaurant, noticing we were the only two left, I laughed and replied, "Sorry, Lynn, we got caught up in the moment enjoying such fine food and ambiance."

Lynn then said, "I kinda think the three bottles of wine might have helped too! Be careful tonight."

Well, I must say, being careful was not on my mind at all.

I don't remember the walk home, but I do remember when we arrived. The subtle moonlight was shining in my bedroom window from across Cudjoe Bay.

Corbett A. Davis Jr.

"Would you like a nightcap or a taste of port, Tracy?" I asked.

As she flipped the bedroom light off, in a very sexy yet vulnerable voice, Tracy answered, "It's not wine that I am interested in tonight, Powell."

I turned quickly with surprise in the darkness toward Tracy's voice. Except for a pair of tiny white lace panties, she stood naked. The pale light from a full moon cast a faint glow across her flawless body. Standing in awe, I was breathless and speechless. This was neither what I expected nor what I wanted, or did I? Thoughts of Dawn dimmed as I shamelessly felt myself smiling. Tracy's slender body and perfect breasts were calling me. She stepped toward me, my mind still spinning. Even being consumed with thoughts of Dawn haunting me, I could not resist. At first I was thinking, "I can't say no." It would hurt her feelings. But I knew that was a lie as I wanted her too. When she got so close that I felt her breath on my neck, I reached out holding her face in my hands. When my lips met hers, she began trembling. Although her body continued to shake, Tracy held on tight to my shoulders. I thought I heard a low pleasurable groan when I reached down to remove her panties. With my hands inside her panties, I let my fingertips slide softly across her smooth skin. The little white lace fell to her ankles. Hot passion and desire was mutual. Our bodies seemed to move with each other's breath and heartbeat.

Tracy broke our kiss and put the side of her face against my lips. With one hand still on my shoulder, the other unsnapped my pants. Then, in one motion with both hands, she removed my shorts and held me tight. Then she looked me in the eyes still stroking me with one palm while her other hand clawed at my back. I pulled my T-shirt over my head and it dropped to the floor covering her white lace panties.

Tracy began nibbling across my chest as if searching with her tongue and teeth. She continued the salacious maneuvers until her knees hit the floor. Her hands were all over my body, first my back, then my thighs. She then grabbed my ass with both hands, and the kissing became licking when she found me with her mouth. Tightening her lips around me, she began to move back and forth. The erotic movements were so passionate I had to stop her. I grabbed her by the shoulders and yanked her to her feet.

Still kissing and clawing like two teenagers in the back seat of daddy's Oldsmobile, Tracy backed me up onto the bed. I lay there hard, erect, and pulsating. Tracy climbed me, with one hand strong on my chest slightly spreading her thighs as she slid smoothly thrusting me inside her. After our eyes met, her head dropped back as she sat upright moving more rapidly, enjoying the pulse of penetration that excited us both. Our rhythm connected, we moved together slipping and sliding as one. Her head fell forward, her fingernails now clawed at my chest. I pulled her close; my tongue found her aroused nipples. Then her body tightened as I thrust upward faster and harder. Her beautiful petite body collapsed onto mine only seconds after moving intensely with me sending the ultimate pleasure throughout my body. I hugged her against my sweaty chest, kissed her neck softly, and we both floated off to sleep.

CHAPTER 25

An unfamiliar, horrific odor filled the dark corridor of the corroded walkways as Dawn searched in blindness for an escape. The smells of rust-covered metal along with antiseptic scents were familiar, but the additional foul stench scared the hell out of her.

"Death!" she thought to herself. "That is what reeks in these halls." A chilling sensation flowed down Dawn's spine, a result no doubt, of being half naked and frightened. But she knew she could not give into her fear. She had to believe that Powell was nearby looking for her. Surely, somehow he figured it all out, and soon, this would all be just a bad memory. These thoughts were all that kept Dawn encouraged for now. Feeling her way through the ship's narrow walkways, she hoped she was headed toward the back of the boat, the stern, as Powell had taught her. The only knowledge Dawn had of boats and the sea came from time spent on the water with Powell.

She was also hoping there would be an exit door at the rear of the ship, the opposite end of the bow. She assumed the captain and crew would be forward, near the bow steering the ship to port. Common sense also told Dawn her direction to the stern was accurate. Earlier, when the boat had abruptly stopped, it almost threw Dawn feet first off the table. She merely followed the direction of her feet. However, a maze of passageways and corridors confused Dawn. Stairwells and ladders, empty old staterooms, and hatches to nowhere made the half-naked, frightened young woman feel totally entrapped. Thinking there is no way out, she fell to the floor sobbing. The uncontrollable tears were running down her face dripping onto her chest. "Damn it, I want some clothes!" she yelled. The echo of her voice startled her at first. She closed her eyes and listened intensely in silence, hoping for a sound, any noise, or maybe a miracle. Then, out of nowhere, she heard it. A low vibrating thud of sounds coming from the direction she was heading caught her attention. She was encouraged for the first time since her imprisonment began. On her feet again, she continued through narrow passages toward the noise. Creeping up and down stairwells, she never stopped to think or try to make any sense of it. The sounds grew louder as Dawn continued. She was getting close now. But what she did not know was the source of the continuous humming noise.

The engine room of the *Lady Demonio* was located aft near the bottom of the rusty vessel. Huge diesel engines that ran the propellers took up much of the room. Besides these engines, the room also contained generators, air compressors, feed pumps, and fuel pumps. Since the diesel engines had been turned off when the ship arrived in Cuba, it was the vibration of the generators that led Dawn down and aft. The starboard generator provided power to exhaust blowers allowing airflow for ventilation. The port generators provided power for the ships electrical systems. A third generator was a backup to ensure smooth operations should one of the others malfunction. Like the immaculate medical rooms, but unlike the rest of the ship, the engine room was very high tech with all of the newest equipment. From climate-controlled devices to electric thrusters for maneuvering and docking, the ship needed to be ready for quick departures if necessary.

When Dawn finally reached the engine room, she saw light bouncing from the hatch opening. Very cautiously, she crept to the door and peeked inside. The sound of the generators and water pouring out of a

Corbett A. Davis Jr.

hose through the hull into the sea were all that could be heard. Dawn was relieved to not hear voices inside. Entering with high hopes, she was scoping out the room like a thief casing out Caribbean Jewelers before a robbery. Her eyes moved left to right searching hard for a door or any kind of escape from this hellhole. On her third scan, reality hit her hard. There was no escape hatch or exit door. As panic set in something caught her eye, a small pair of bunk beds in the back corner. On the top bunk was a pile of freshly folded laundry. Dawn was more than pleasantly surprised at what joy this sight brought to her. Winning the lottery could not have made her happier. The men's medium boxer shorts and a large white T-shirt would not set a fashion trend but felt like heaven as she slipped into them.

"If only I had a hot bath and some good fried yellowtail snapper, beans, and rice and a cold beer!" She thought as she choked back the tears again.

CHAPTER 26

I did not wait for the alarm clock this morning. It was not necessary. Between the guilt I felt over my sexual activity last night and the anticipation of entering Cuba, I did not sleep at all. I only hoped that this sleep deprivation would not hurt me in the hours ahead.

I managed to slip out of bed without waking Tracy. The pitch black of midnight still lingered at four fifteen. A hint of moonlight remained, reflecting across the sheets accenting Tracy's cute little round, smooth ass. Seeing her lying there naked, so beautiful and inviting, was arousing. For a moment, I considered slipping back into the covers and repeating last night's sensual rendezvous. But I knew Limbo would be arriving in forty-five minutes, ready to go. Besides, he would demand an explanation and wonder what the hell I was thinking.

The guilt of betrayal hit me like a ton of bricks as I considered the thought of Dawn's return. "How could I possibly have let that happen last night?" came to my mind. Then I remembered what started it all. Those bottles of good wine and a blowjob are powerful weapons and excellent persuaders. That reminded me of something I read back in my college days. Big Jim Folsom, the six foot eight inch sinful and colorful Governor of Alabama, once said during his early years in office, "Bait the trap with pussy and whiskey, and you're gonna catch Big Jim every time."

I hate to think I'm no different. Bait the trap with a good blowjob along with three bottles of Jarvis Cabernet and Ole Powell will sin with the best of them. The gloom of my guilt now returned with the thought of sunlight. This was not what I had in mind for my vowed reform.

I scribbled a quick note of thanks to Tracy telling her good-bye. Although she knew I would be gone for a while to Cuba, she simply thought it was a routine fishing trip. I saw no reason for further explanation, especially when it concerned my search for Dawn and what she meant to me. It was just too complicated.

By the time Limbo arrived, the caffeine buzz from the Cuban coffee along with a heavy dose of an adrenaline rush had me bouncing off the walls. I did not see a need to mention Tracy to Limbo. Fearing she may stumble out of the bedroom naked any minute, I grabbed two cups of the strong coffee and hurried Limbo to the skiff.

The bright orange influence from the rising sun mirrored on a catfish moon's surface. This was the very same full-moon phase that old-timers swore created the perfect tide for catching big fish. I hoped and prayed that the old tale was also true about catching villainous slime like those that had apparently kidnapped Dawn. From the boat, we both watched in silence as the moon set at precisely the same time as the sun rose. "That's magical," Limbo muttered.

As we idled quietly down the canal, I turned on the GPS, watching as the screen lit up with a programmed course that I had just entered yesterday. The compass heading of 203 degrees indicated ninety-eight and one-half miles to Marina Hemingway in Cuba. The weather conditions could have been more favorable for the start of our journey. Inside the reef, we pounded through two- to three-foot waves knowing it would probably get worse before it got better. The forecast called for a fifteen- to twenty-knot wind out of the southeast with four- to five-foot seas outside the reef. However, the weather report also said that by later today, the seas would calm down and be flat and glassy, continuing through our return trip in a few days. That was news that both Limbo and I were happy to hear. When we passed the American Shoal tower, the seas were easily four to five feet now as we crossed the reef. Slowing our speed, with every bounce, we slammed hard on the next wave. My rib cage and abs were sore from my recent workouts. The pain in my muscles was now screaming to me that the exercise was working. I hoped Lorenzo would appreciate it. Maybe my trophy T-shirt was not far away. But the muscle burn felt good.

About a mile south of the reef tower, the engine alarm sounded. I threw the throttle into neutral as I tried to maneuver the skiff through rough seas.

"What the fuck, Powell?" Limbo screamed.

The now-struggling sunrise was obscured by some dark ominous clouds on the eastern horizon. Just as I was thinking that maybe the weather forecast was incorrect, the annoying loud pitch of the engine's alarm snapped me back to the present. Was the outboard getting oil? Did it overheat? Or was it just an omen of more bad things to come? Had Limbo known what was packed in our gear he would have said, "It's those fucking bananas!" Even I started to wonder.

We had just crossed a weed line, so I hoped the outboard had sucked up some grass into the intake creating the noise. I put the engine in reverse for a few seconds and then back into neutral. The alarm ceased, and we thankfully continued on our journey. As the waves grew stronger, I could not help but to think of those damn bananas. Surely, it was folklore. How could it possibly be true? No, of course not. I refused to believe in bad luck.

By the time we were fifteen miles offshore, the wind had picked up, and the seas were now six to seven feet. Right ahead, we saw an obvious sargasso weed line. As we crossed the seaweed, the water color instantly

Corbett A. Davis Jr.

changed to a beautiful and crystal clear dark indigo blue. We were now in the Gulf Stream, a river that flowed within the ocean. Running east-northeast, it flows at different speeds within its stream and careful calculations are critical when tracking through it, especially with no GPS (Global Positioning Satellite). The Gulf Stream is capable of pushing you off course to the east by many miles. It surges through the Florida Straits at three knots or more. Without a GPS setting, a heading of ten to twenty degrees west of your compass heading is often necessary to maintain course to compensate for the currents. Today, the wind was howling from the east and southeast while the current of the Gulf Stream was traveling east-northeast. Opposing winds and currents made for very choppy and rough conditions, especially in a sixteen-foot flats skiff.

I did not have the luxury to think of Dawn, nor did I have time to further discuss plans with Limbo. I was busy keeping the bow of the skiff above water. We were twenty miles offshore, and the seas were at least seven feet now. I realized for the first time that the marine forecast had been seriously wrong. The winds were increasing, not lying down as predicted. This concerned me. We were sloshing around in a huge washing machine, trying hard to keep course.

Pointing to the sky ahead where a frigate bird hovered above, Limbo said, "Let's catch a big dolphin to take to Cuba. The Cuban officials at the dock would love some fresh mahi-mahi for dinner tonight. Besides, it might make our entry into the communist country a little easier"

Despite the rough seas, I agreed and opened the rod locker where I had stored a small flagpole with two flags for our arrival at Marina Hemingway. The top flag was the flag of Cuba, and below it was the yellow quarantine flag. Both were required for entry into Cuban waters.

I moved the flags aside, grabbed a spinning rod rigged for dolphin, and handed it to Limbo. Limbo let out line as I followed the path of seaweed and the lone frigate bird. The boat was rocking from side to side taking on water. It was not long before Limbo's rod bent double and the acrobatic dance of a fifteen-pound dolphin began. The iridescent green and gold on the skin of the fish disappeared behind the crests of the now eight-foot seas. That is when I first heard the painful sound that I would hear too many more times before this long day would end. Limbo was bent over the side of the skiff heaving his breakfast into the gulf waters. I grabbed the rod with my left hand jerking the fish into the boat as my right hand was almost numb from squeezing the steering wheel so hard while trying to get the boat back up on plane.

Seasickness is a feeling that is hard to explain to someone who has never experienced it. The closest comparison might be a hangover after a three week drinking binge.

Limbo asked if I minded if he drove the boat with hopes of taking his mind off the sickness. I jumped up and gladly handed the wheel over, knowing he was capable, even if sick. But we would not fish again on this day or this trip.

Corbett A. Davis Jr.

CHAPTER 27

As we plowed through the turbulent seas, I had visions of walking the streets of old Havana while sipping a mojito and smoking a fat Cuban cigar on the back lawn of Hotel Nationale. But I knew that would probably not happen on this trip. We had a different mission to accomplish, and it was one of importance that was filled with danger. Plus, time was running out. A brief moment reminiscing of good memories with Dawn abruptly halted when I noted the GPS had lost power. Another omen, I thought. Then I remembered the bananas. Limbo slowed the boat trying hard to keep it afloat while I stuck my head under the console. I was able to reconnect some wiring rendering the GPS operational again.

"What luck!" Limbo exclaimed.

Luck indeed, I thought. If only he knew about the bananas. The water continued to build, still hitting us from the southeast on our port side. There were no words spoken for the next hour and a half. I knew Limbo must have been as uncomfortable as I was in these conditions. We were powering up the front of each wave and slamming down the backside, taking water over the bow with each hit. It took skillful maneuvering on Limbo's part just to keep us afloat. Just as I was thinking how I could crawl to the forward hatch, retrieve my bag, and slip the bananas overboard unnoticed, he said, as if reading my mind, "You sure you didn't bring any fucking bananas, Powell?"

I just gave him a disgusted look and shook my head. Surely, they could not be the reason for such bad luck.

At sixty-two miles offshore and only thirty-eight and a half miles from Marina Hemingway and Dawn, we hit what must have been the axis of the Gulf Stream. Before we could adjust, the skiff began to bounce around like a buoy in the high seas with some waves as high as twelve feet. And the bad thing was, these huge walls of water had no rhythm or pattern to them. Waves crashed from all directions. They pounded head on, and then came from the port or starboard. Next, we found ourselves surfing straight down the face of a wave that hit from behind. Finally, I said, "The hell with it, I had to get rid of the bad juju. No use in tempting fate. It may only be superstition, but why chance it?" Between the pounding and tumult of the disoriented wave action, I managed to crawl to the forward hatch and retrieve my bag. I unzipped the side compartment and removed the cursed fruit. Just when I went to slip them overboard, discreetly without Limbo's knowledge, a twelve-foot rogue wave hit the stern of the boat slamming the skiff downward. The skiff crashed at the bottom of the wave with such power that I dropped the contraband. I was violently tossed overboard and as if in slow motion the two bananas went airborne suspended in air. They hung there for what seemed like minutes as Limbo watched with an expressionless and unexpected awe.

"You son of a bitch," he screamed before realizing the danger I was in.

The same jolt that threw me overboard was destructive enough to also rip the console loose from the deck of the skiff. In a flats boat like the Maverick, the console not only holds all of the steering mechanism and electrical wiring, it is also the only place for a passenger to hold on. With no power or steering Limbo was dead in the water, helpless as waves over the bow filled the skiff. I was swimming frantically toward Limbo and the boat. At times between waves, the skiff disappeared so I could only swim hard toward Limbo's frantic screams. Then out of nowhere, a rope appeared from the sky. Somehow Limbo, while being tossed around in ten-foot seas, managed to tie together some dock lines. I grabbed the rope and pulled myself toward the bouncing skiff. I slammed my rib cage into the gunwale as Limbo helped me aboard. Without a word, we tried to regroup. Sloshing around in knee-deep seawater, I hooked up wires and connected steering cables while Limbo lodged an ice chest between the gunwale and console. With the dock lines, we were able to secure the console to outside cleats. We both were surprised when the engine fired up on the first try. Limbo took the helm, pointed the bow into the waves and slowly got us up on plane. The water inside the boat began to slowly drain, but random waves continued to crash over the bow and fill the skiff again.

"Take the wheel, Powell," Limbo screamed as he began to vomit over the side once more.

All I could think of at the moment was about Limbo's good buddy, Adm. Robert Papp. I was even thinking it in Limbo lingo. "Fuck the Coast Guard, Customs, and the Homeland Security."

With no GPS, I kept us on course with the compass, which I hoped was still functional and accurate.

Limbo washed his face with seawater and said, "If my calculations are correct, we are about twenty miles from Havana, and in these conditions, we have enough fuel to cover twenty four miles. We have no room for error. Keep the heading as close to 203 degrees as possible. With this wind and current, we should make it to the marina in about two hours."

A short time later, the wind and the seas calmed somewhat. With Limbo at the wheel again, I was now able to crawl to the forward hatch and retrieve the handheld GPS.

"If you pull another fucking banana out of there, I'll throw your ass overboard myself and pick you up on the way back," Limbo said without the slightest hint of a grin.

I ignored him, but it was interesting that as soon as the bananas were gone our luck seemed to change for the better. I would never admit it that to Limbo. We were now in two- to three-foot seas, and the Havana skyline was in sight. I turned on the GPS to surprisingly find out we were only eight miles from Marina Hemingway. The relief and joy I felt for a brief moment was immediately replaced with the painful reality of the situation. As soon as we passed through the jetties outside of the marina, we saw it. A vision of a red cross on the ship's bow, anchored offshore, slammed me back into reality. Our voyage was over but the journey was about to begin. The reason for this trip seemed more urgent than ever. I could not, nor did I want to, imagine what Dawn might be going through.

CHAPTER 28

When Dawn first heard the men's voices, it startled her. She was numb, trying to listen, trying to digest. More importantly, she was trying to determine the direction they were coming from. Instinct finally kicked in. She opened the hatch, leaped out in the opposite direction of the approaching men, and ducked into a dark hole of an opening. The room was freezing cold and reeked of an even more rancid odor than before. As the constant, rapid chatter seemed to close in, Dawn ducked farther back into the shadows. Although speaking a language she did not recognize, the tone and pitch of the men told her they were very agitated. The unrecognizable yelling convinced Dawn they were pissed off beyond comprehension. She suspected it might have something to do with her escape from the hospital bed.

What Dawn did not know was that if the men did not find her, and find her quickly, the two Muslims would be beheaded, their organs harvested and sold to the highest bidder. There was quite an incentive for the killers to be successful.

The closer the men's voices got, the deeper into the dark cabin compartment Dawn crawled. The air was pitch black and was thick with stench of death and decay. Holding her nose and trying to fight the tears, Dawn continued to move back. Experiencing fear like she had never known, she hit the rear wall with nowhere else to hide. Dawn closed her eyes listening keenly, trying hard to determine the location of the two approaching voices. The talking suddenly stopped. The squeaks she now heard in her ears were playing tricks on her. She leaned sideways, banging the top of her head as if trying to clear water from her ears. The squeaks continued louder and louder. It was not until she felt something move and scurry across her foot did she realize she was not alone. In her imagination, she could picture hundreds of rats hiding in the dark feeding on the flesh of other dead decaying rats. She became nauseous at the thought. The distinct foul smell was obviously coming from the rat carcasses. It was a recognizable smell she remembered from her early teens when her cat had been missing for a week. Dawn tried to think of more pleasant thoughts. She remembered that when she had found her rotting cat the odor caused her to violently vomit. She could not allow that to happen now. The noise would surely alert the two men searching for her. Suffering silently in pain, her body convulsed with spasmodic contractions.

Dawn heard the voices and knew the men were close. Holding her breath, she slowly opened her eyes and looked around. The darkness gave her no relief. A beam from the distant flashlight partially lit up the room where Dawn hid. The morbid sight was more than she could handle. The loud, raging, spewing of vomit surely had to alert the two men, she thought. But it was unavoidable. The light's beam had uncovered the source of the putrid smell. It was not rat carcasses as she had incorrectly assumed. In this room of horror deep in the bottom of the ship were mutilated and rotting human bodies. The convulsions and spasms now were joined with tears and uncontrollable crying. Dawn's exhausted body was too spent to recover. Knowing she was defeated and beat down, she gave in to her own fatigue.

When the two men with flashlights entered the chamber, blinding her, she lay motionless as tears rolled down her cheeks. They were surprisingly gentle as they escorted her up the many flights of stairs.

Corbett A. Davis Jr.

They stripped her naked, cleaned her body, and washed and towel-dried her hair before strapping her down again on the hospital bed. They then covered her nude body with linen sheets. As if in a trance, Dawn was like a zombie obeying the call of the walking dead. She knew there was no hope now. Having given up completely, she closed her eyes and began her act of contrition.

"Oh my god, I am heartily sorry for having offended thee and I—" was all she recited before the cold needle pierced her upper arm.

Once again Dawn's beautiful yet frail nude body was unconscious on a cold hospital bed. But this time, unknown to her, she was not on a bed at all. Time was running out, as she lay motionless on the operating table.

CHAPTER 29

Clearing customs and immigration in Cuba was painless and quick. The fact that Limbo could speak fluent Spanish seemed to help. And he asked them to not stamp our passports, which fortunately met no resistance. We were well prepared for the unique requirements to get into Cuba and had all of our documents filled out in advance.

When we pulled the single dolphin from the cooler and presented it to Adolpho, the officer in charge, he was visibly pleased. His grin broke into loud laughter as Limbo explained that we would have brought more, but he was too busy vomiting from seasickness. I assumed that our humble approach must have been refreshing to the Cuban officials. Maybe our great respect of Cuban culture was apparent. It is not unrealistic to believe that most American tourists visiting Cuba come across as arrogant, wealthy, better than thou, and pains in the asses. However, Adolpho seemed to really like us. He helped over fill our fuel tanks and secure the skiff. Not knowing how or when we would be leaving the island, the boat had to be ready in case we needed to exit quickly. And thanks to our new Cuban friend, grabbing a taxi to our hotel was effortless. The Spanish-speaking driver dropped us off in front of the impressive hotel Habana Libre. Originally named the Havana Hilton, the name changed in 1960 when all American owned hotels were nationalized under the new communist government.

Suite 2324 served as Fidel Castro's private headquarters in 1959 when he first entered Havana. There were large photos in the lobby of him with

Che Guevara. Both were dressed in camo holding assault rifles with the caption "Revolution."

Hotel Habana Libre, Havana's largest hotel, was the perfect choice for our stay. With five hundred seventy-one rooms, all with balconies, the one hundred thirty dollars for a room and a great breakfast buffet seemed reasonable. However, we did not decide to stay here for the breakfast, the second floor swimming pool or the Cabaret Turquino on the twenty-fifth floor. We stayed here for the same reasons most foreign journalists and Europeans often do. Besides convenience, the hotel is useful for its many amenities including a telephone center, photo service, shops, and a taxi stand. Had I been visiting Cuba under different circumstances, I would have preferred Hotel Nationale. Overlooking the Malecon (Havana's seawall along the coast), Hotel Nationale with its surprisingly large plain rooms is quite a tourist destination. Famous former guests include Winston Churchill, Ava Gardner, and Frank Sinatra, who attended a mafia reunion there in 1946.

A fan of Ernest Hemingway, I wished I had time to retrace all off his Cuban tracks.

"My daiquiris at La Floridita and my mojitoes at La Bodequita del Medio" were famous words that Papa Hemingway often mumbled incoherently after a busy night on the streets of old Habana.

I have always had a thirst for more knowledge about Cuba and her people and now found myself a bit distracted from the mission at hand. But as Limbo told me, "Powell, forget it, we're here for more important fucking reasons!"

Limbo has such a command on the English vocabulary.

By the time we arrived at our hotel, darkness had settled over Havana. The taxi ride form Marina Hemingway took less than twenty minutes.

After seeing the *Lady Demonia* anchored near the harbor, an adrenaline rush forced much needed glucose and oxygen to my brain.

"Let's hurry up, Limbo, and get out there. Time is ticking away! If she is still alive, I know Dawn is in great danger. I'm ready to kick some ass and get her out of there," I said rather loudly.

"Calm down, Powell," Limbo answered. "We can't just rush in, grab Dawn, and jump overboard," he continued.

"Why not?" I replied.

"Powell, we need a sensible plan, one that will save Dawn, and keep us breathing too," Limbo said with a smirk.

Since we had not eaten or slept much, we decided to get a quick dinner, take a short nap, and get up at 1:00 a.m. to plan our attack.

After a very fast check-in, we dropped off our luggage, and I talked Limbo into dining at La Floridita. Typical tourists, we had the Papa Hemingway daiquiris, the favorite Papa and Mary entree of grilled fish, shrimp, and crabmeat and finally finished with a great homemade flan. The 1952 Chevy taxi we hailed to take us back to our hotel seemed as big as my living room back on Cudjoe. We had the overly friendly Cuban driver drop us off three blocks before the hotel. He was extremely grateful for the meager five-dollar tip.

On each street corner, small trios of local musicians were playing typical Cuban tunes. Kids were dancing in the street, playing baseball, and riding bicycles. It was 8:00 p.m., and Havana was alive with excitement and tradition. "What a beautiful country with such beautiful people," I thought. Extraordinary architecture from a past era was now crumbling. The people seemed poor financially but very rich in life and spirit. I saw no fancy cars, cell phones, laptops, iPads, or iPods, but the streets were full of people, music, and history. I suppose you don't miss what you've never had. It was refreshing and brought back fond memories from my

Corbett A. Davis Jr.

childhood before we had any of the finer things in life. For a moment, I missed those simpler days.

"Hurry up, Powell, we have work to do!" Limbo snapped.

I was able to get about four-and-a-half-hours of sleep before the 1:00 a.m. alarm sounded. Limbo was sitting at the kitchen table with a cup of coffee he made, scribbling on a notepad. On one page, he had made a list of anything and everything he thought we would need aboard the ship. From guns, ammo, and knives to flashlights and our watches, he seemed to have thought of everything. On another sheet, Limbo had sketched out a diagram of a ship similar to the *Demonio* vessel with the Red Cross logo that he had googled earlier in the week.

I poured myself a cup of potent coffee and joined Limbo at the table. Renderings from Limbo's Google search similar to our demon ship showed two easily accessible hatches. One entry was aft on the port side while the other was forward on the starboard. Hopefully, one or both would have rope ladders that hang down to the water's surface. We both agreed we would be lucky if either was there. It was a very hot and humid evening outside tonight. A typical summer Cuban night, the light from a big moon along with the light pollution from Havana's skyline would likely make us more visible on the water. We both dressed in all dark clothing of long pants, ski masks, black shirts, and tennis shoes.

Limbo discussed different approaches and scenarios depending on the conditions we would find once we arrived. The ship was anchored with the bow into the wind facing East with the stern due west. The best case scenario would be for us to run the skiff around to the north side of the ship. This would shield us from most of the light coming from Havana and keep us less visible. The north side of the ship would be the port side and we could hopefully climb the rope ladder near the stern. This would not be an easy task since we would be carrying full backpacks with guns, knives, ammo, and flashlights. A familiar chill ran up my spine as I thought how slim our chances were to find and save Dawn.

"Let's go, Limbo!" I shouted.

Limbo quickly agreed.

We strolled through the hotel's lobby to meet our taxicab. The ballroom was alive with music and dance with ladies in flowing gowns gliding across the dance floor with dapper partners in tailed tuxedos. It was not exactly the picture that I had previously imagined of this third-world communist country and its ruthless dictator. I could feel the energy in the room as happiness bounced from every wall. The elegant scene captured my attention, and I hoped that we would later have cause for celebration and be able to enjoy this local Cuban backdrop.

Most of the archaic streetlights in Marina Hemingway were burned out, casting dark shadows on our sixteen-foot skiff when we arrived.

Once we cleared the mouth of the marina and entered the gulf, I was able to use the flashlight. The subtle beam allowed us to access the hidden locker and remove our weapons. I grabbed one of the knives and the twelve gauge. Limbo put a knife in his backpack and took the Glock and Sig semiautomatic.

Between the moon and the light cast from Havana, the ship stood out like the *Titanic* in a Hollywood scene. The light winds and calm seas made it easy for us to maneuver the skiff to the port side. As we approached, I felt the frightening spirits of the *Lady Demonia* the same way as the Key West tourist must have felt when she first arrived in that southernmost city. Once we cleared the stern, we were hidden from view by the huge vessel. The hatch was just where Limbo had predicted it would be. Aft, only forty feet from the stern, we saw a beautiful and comforting sight. The rope ladder hung on the rusty hull like a fisherman's cast net.

Slowly and carefully, I eased the skiff forward as Limbo tied a bowline to the ladders rope. We had no idea as to what we would find.

CHAPTER 30

The mysterious *Star of Ashrafi* did not seem to attract the degree of attention from the Cuban population as it did with the tourists of Key West. In fact, no one seemed to even notice the rusty vessel anchored just outside the harbor only two hundred feet from shore. For a ship the size of this one, she had a very small crew. The only people aboard the boat now besides Dawn were the captain, his copilot, two crew members, and the remaining five-person medical team. Assisting the surgeon would be two nurses, one male and one female; an anesthesiologist; and a security guard who was also trained in the transport of human organs. The other donors' remains, along with Dr. Shezad's body, had already been thrown down in the aft pit on the starboard side where Dawn had recently been recaptured. The two men about to board would soon reduce the number of survivors on the ship. Unfortunately, Dawn's chances of living diminished with each passing minute.

The captain and copilot were forward in the pilothouse awaiting instructions to pull anchor and head to sea. The two crew members were resting in their bunks in the engine room port side near the stern. The security officer was moving throughout the ship securing each floor. All was quiet aboard at the moment. But things can certainly change very quickly.

Midship on the port side in the cold, sterile, high-tech operating room, there was much activity. The nurses were preparing the room as they set up and cleaned the surgical instruments. The anesthesiologist had already started the IV drip in Dawn's frail arm while the Mideastern surgeon marked Dawn's chest with precise incision lines using a black marker. The room was now ready. The medical team was ready to harvest Dawn's heart for the survival of the son of Iran's wealthy Shah. As soon as the security guard arrived with the special organ transport chest, the doctor would initiate the procedure.

At 4:00 a.m., in the dark of night, a helicopter would land on the deck of the ship and pick up the security guard along with Dawn's heart. A fueled private jet waited at Havana's Jose Marti International Airport. As soon as the heart was safely secured aboard the helicopter, the ship would be under way. The plan was to pull anchor at 3:45 a.m. The helicopter would land at four and would leave the deck at four fifteen after the precious cargo had been delivered. The *Star of Ashrafi* would immediately set sail for the Dominican Republic while the Iranian jet would fly all night to Paris. One of the best surgical teams money could buy would be standing by to receive the heart. The Shah's son was resting in his private room soon to be prepared for heart surgery.

Meanwhile, Dawn's consciousness flickered on and off like a loose light bulb. When she would awake, she kept her eyes closed, listening closely, concentrating on voices and noises while hoping to catch a clue. She waited desperately for some explanation of what was happening. She knew she was in danger and would most likely not survive this. Dawn heard the hatch door open as someone entered and mumbled a few words to the others in the room. From the voice, she only knew that it was a man. What she did not know was that the security officer had finished his rounds, checking the entire ship. He now stood two feet from Dawn's side holding a large high-tech-looking insulated box.

Corbett A. Davis Jr.

Lying there terrified and barely breathing with her eyes tightly shut, there was no way for her to know what the briefcase sized box meant. She would never have the luxury of finding out. Still somewhat experimental, it was the latest in German technology. This organ-care system keeps donor hearts functioning while they are transported in a sterile chamber to the fortunate recipient. The heart is connected at the aorta, the pulmonary artery, and the left atrium, allowing it to be fed with oxygenated and nutrient rich blood from the donor at body temperature. This system is able to keep a heart alive for twelve to fourteen hours. The flight from Havana to Paris would take ten hours. Before this process, donated hearts were cooled with ice, deteriorating rapidly, and giving surgeons only four hours between their harvest and their implantation into recipients. Although the new system makes the operation less pressured for time, it does not make any difference in the number of hearts available. And that is precisely why Dawn lay here now on the operating table, less than an hour from having her heart stolen.

At 3:00 a.m., the last time Dawn felt that she would ever open her eyes again, her questions were answered. Looking down at her body, she saw the sheet pulled down below her breasts. The frightening black lines painted on her chest told the whole story. Dawn could no longer hold on. Her involuntary sobbing alerted the nurses and within a few seconds a warm sensation filled her veins. But before the fast-acting sedative Versed put Dawn to sleep forever, she pleaded with her god in a last prayer.

"Please, God, save me from this nightmare. Take me now, and let me die in peace and join you for eternity."

Her prayer was answered.

CHAPTER 31

Like Jack and the Beanstalk, Limbo and I climbed toward the heavens wondering just what evil giants awaited us. Scaling the rope with a full backpack was not an easy task for me. Limbo crawled it quickly and effortlessly as I whipped around like a fly on a horse's tail. Finally reaching the hatch opening, Limbo cheerfully greeted me, "It's about fucking time!"

Even in the most dangerous of times, Limbo's vocabulary is predictable.

As we had carefully discussed earlier, I was simply following Limbo's instructions. He had experience and history dealing with such clandestine situations. I did not. I only hoped for luck. His instincts would be the best and our only chance for the possibility of rescuing Dawn and saving ourselves.

A glow from my watch brightened the darkness. The luminous digits on my stainless steel Rolex Submariner, a gift from my father, Charles Sr., lit up the black dial. Easily readable, it showed exactly 1:45 a.m. For some reason, my mind drifted off to a time long ago when I was eagerly studying and working in my father's jewelry store back in Gulf Breeze. The much older edition watch dial glowed more in the dark than newer models like my current watch. Before World War II, radium was used on watch dials. Radio luminescence would glow in the dark without any exposure to light as it was produced by nuclear radiation. Gamma and X-rays were used to excite the electrons in a radio luminescent compound such as zinc sulfide. This type of material was used in watches for more than seventy-five years. Today, the radiation can be harmful and it is prohibited in watches and clocks.

"Clocks! What the fuck are you mumbling about over there, Powell? Pay attention. We're not in a goddamn jewelry store. We're on a ship fighting for your girlfriend's fucking life," Limbo snapped.

I worried just what had triggered that untimely recollection. Fear or sadness maybe. More likely, it was guilt. If and when I made it back to Key West, I would call home and check on my dad and my family.

Following Limbo, both of us armed with guns and knives, we were headed in the direction of the stern. Limbo wanted to locate the engine room before we searched for Dawn. He would stop occasionally and check his googled diagram with the flashlight before continuing on. After ten or fifteen minutes, I heard voices that Limbo obviously did not. When I grabbed his arm, he turned quickly. Before he could spit out what probably would have started with the F-word, I put my finger to my lips and whispered, "Voices."

He turned and nodded his head in agreement.

By the time we reached the open hatch of the engine room, the voices were loud with laughter. We stood in the hallway darkness for a moment while Limbo studied their behavior. Lying on their bunks the two Mideastern men laughed hysterically.

"They're drunk," Limbo quickly murmured.

Then he smiled as if he had a great idea. And to my surprise, Limbo stood up tall and just walked through the door opening and shouted, "Hello, gentlemen."

I followed closely.

The two men were so startled that the one on the lower bunk jumped fast, smashing his head on the upper bunk rail. The man on the top bunk slipped off the bed, fell to the floor, and hit the steel hull with a loud thud. The head injuries of both men seemed to sober them instantly. By the time they were on their feet and before they could grab a weapon, Limbo was in their face.

Surprisingly, my fear was gone, replaced with confidence and strength, allowing me to actually help Limbo in this dangerous situation. Limbo grabbed the larger man around the neck and began to struggle. Just as the other man managed to locate his pistol and turn to find Limbo's head, I buried the seven-inch filet knife into the side of his neck. An awful gasping sound along with a steady flow of blood gushing from the hole left by the serrated blade managed to get Limbo's attention.

Still in one-on-one combat, he managed to turn my way. As I was about to stick my knife into the neck of our second enemy, Limbo yelled, "NO! I want him alive."

I picked his buddy's pistol up from the floor and stuck it into the man's ear. He ceased to struggle immediately. In very bad English, he said, "'Kay, you win," and held up his hands.

From a spool of heavy rope that Limbo found, he tied the man up. Limbo used the strong pipes and metal from the exposed ship's engine to secure him. Tied at both hands, both feet and the neck, there would be no chance of escape. Limbo dragged the blood-drained body of his friend over and placed him as his feet. The man refused to look. Limbo took my knife and held it to the surviving Muslim's throat and began to ask questions.

Limbo started with, "Answer my questions, and you will live. Don't cooperate, and you will meet Allah a few minutes after your friend here."

As he pointed the knife blade at the head of his dead partner, it took all of about six minutes at best for the scared wretch to spill his guts. With

Corbett A. Davis Jr.

all the information he now needed, Limbo tied an old shirt tight around the man's head and mouth to keep him muffled.

After a few basic questions, we now knew where the dead bodies were stored, how many people were on board, and where they all were. We also learned that there was also a strong possibility that Dawn was already dead. The man told Limbo that her heart would be transported by helicopter at 4:00 a.m. He did not know any other arrangements. Feeling sick to my stomach, I looked down at my watch and told Limbo, "Two forty-five."

"We have to hurry," he replied.

Limbo found a toolbox and began looking through it for something.

"What are you doing?" I yelled frantically.

"What we came to the engine room for," he replied without looking up. "Oh yeah! That will work great," he continued as he held up an electric drill with about a quarter-inch bit.

Limbo went over to the ship's engine and studied it for a minute. He drilled what seemed to be five or six holes into some pipes. Then Limbo found some old rags and clothing that he tied to both engines near the holes he had drilled.

Limbo looked at me and said, "We need to find Dawn quickly. I know where she is, and it will take us ten minutes to get there. But if for any reason the captain starts the engines, we need to get off the boat as soon as possible, with or without Dawn, understood?"

"No! I do not understand Limbo," I said. "What the hell are you talking about with or without Dawn?"

"I'll explain while we run through the halls towards the operating room."

It took him about half the distance to Dawn's room to fill me in. When the ships engines are started, diesel fuel and fumes will spew from the holes he drilled in the fuel line and exhaust pipes. The gas will soak the rags that are tied to the engines manifold within ten to twelve minutes, depending on RPMs and throttle speed. The manifold will get red hot, and then the rags will combust. It will take another three or four minutes to ignite the fuel tanks. A moment later the explosion that occurs will not only light up the Gulf of Mexico but will also sink the ship in a matter of seconds.

"We'll have seventeen or eighteen minutes tops to escape before we become char grilled," warned Limbo.

It was quiet when we approached the operating room where Dawn was being held captive.

"It's too fucking quiet. That's not good at all." Limbo whispered.

And then things got worse. One at a time, the ships two engines fired up. We were twelve minutes from the rope ladder to my skiff and about seventeen minutes before the anticipated explosion. We had only five minutes to find and save Dawn. We had no time to spare by getting lost, by wasting time, or by engaging in further combat.

The hatch door opened and out ran a man with an oversized briefcase. A man and a woman followed closely behind.

Limbo pulled out the Glock and told me, "Stay here, I'll be right back!"

He was up and through the hatch opening before I could respond. I heard three shots and took off racing in their direction with a gun in my hands. I should have listened to Limbo and stayed behind. When I arrived, I saw an armed man with head wounds in doctors' scrubs lying dead on the floor.

Limbo bent over a cold steel table, felt my presence, and looked up. I knew from the tears in his eyes what lay beneath the blooded sheets. We were too late.

Limbo pushed me back out of the room and yelled, "We have to hurry. We have less than fifteen minutes before the boat blows."

"What about Dawn?" I pleaded, already knowing the answer.

"I'm sorry, Powell. She's gone, and we need to save ourselves," Limbo answered.

The thirteen-minute run back to the rope ladder where we entered was foggy. All I could think about was Dawn's cold body left behind. Blurring my vision, tears flowed down my face. How did I let this happen? I thought.

The first explosion brought me out of my catatonic state. Staring at the open hatch, Limbo yelled, "Jump now!"

He then leaped as far out as he could. As soon as he hit the water, I followed. Another explosion shook the ship. We swam to the skiff, jumped aboard, and cut the rope to the ladder. I pushed the nose of the skiff north toward Florida and hit the throttle. The bow jumped up on plane in the calm seas, and we were out of sight in seconds. I pulled back on the throttle and idled offshore hidden in darkness. Limbo pointed at the burning ship as a helicopter frantically tried to land on the deck. Now, completely engulfed in flames, I was sure the pilot had orders not to leave without the insulated container that held my Dawn's special heart. I was sick now, bent over the side of the Maverick, splashing saltwater in my face. Limbo gasped as I looked up just in time to see the final blast. It was a magnificent eruption that lit up the Havana skyline, igniting the entire ship, helicopter, and all aboard.

I would later find out there would be no survivors. I was not sad to hear that. To ease some of my guilt and sadness, I would also read later in the *Miami Herald* that the body of Abdul Mutaar washed up on the jetties near Marina Hemingway. The cause of death was from an explosion on the ship *Lady Demonio*, owned by Adbul Mutaar, and fueled by a diesel gas leak in the engine room. By the time Cuban divers were able to explore the wreck, any and all evidence of our involvement was gone. The local Cuban newspaper reported that an Iranian tanker caught fire and exploded last night in the Habana Harbor killing at least twenty people. The list included the owner Abdul Mutaar, a helicopter pilot, and eighteen others, including a twenty-eight-year-old blonde from Florida named Dawn Landry.

CHAPTER 32

The journey back across the Florida Straits to Key West was uneventful and easy. There was no sign of the Coast Guard or Customs to inspect us or welcome us back home. Admiral Papp had kept his end of the bargain.

The flat, calm waters at 4:00 a.m. along with a light south breeze on our stern made for a quick trip. At seven forty-five, I was pulling into the boat slip under my house on Cudjoe Key. We had watched the sun come up from offshore near the reef at American Shoal. With all that had happened in the last couple of days, this sunrise did not seem important. I felt tired, drained, and guilty, but most of all, I felt scared. I would never see Dawn's face again and would always wonder what pain and torture she endured. And it would be a long time before my self-loathing went away. How many times in the coming nights would I lie in bed thinking about what I should have and could have done to prevent this?

For the next few days, Limbo stayed at my house. We talked about our trip to Cuba and how we did all we could have done. We revisited it each and every morning.

Although I had promised nurse Garcia I would call her and give her the news on Dawn, I decided not to. In this case, no news was better than the truth.

After a three long weeks, the pain began to subside slightly. Trying to get my mind off of this tragedy, I had called Tracy a couple times but just was not able to resume a relationship. I told her I wanted to see her but not yet. She knew nothing but still said she understood.

"I'll be here when you're ready, Powell," she told me.

On a Thursday night after dinner at Hogfish Grill on Stock Island and before Limbo disappeared for three days, we had another serious talk.

"Powell, if I die in any mysterious way, promise me no autopsy. I don't want anybody looking at my life history under a microscope," he said.

"What the hell you mean, Limbo?" I replied.

"Well, I've done some crazy shit in my life. Some of the evidence probably still lingers in my blood. I'm almost sixty years old. I've survived STDs, LSD, and a shit pile of other drugs and diseases. I've been with hookers, wives, and ex-wives. No telling what's in my blood stream. Hell, now I take little blue pills occasionally to make my dick hard. The last think I want is some pathologist cutting into my limp body seeing my stiff dick and having blue blood come gushing out. How embarrassing would that be, death by erection!"

"I have no idea what you are talking about Limbo," I said as I got up to get another beer. "All this talk about your death is not healthy and frankly I'm tired of listening to you."

"Powell, I agree. No more talk of my death. But remember, no fucking autopsies!"

We both smiled, and Limbo disappeared into the night.

After calling him for four days with no answer on his cell phone, I finally reached him.

"Hello!" he said in a joyful tone.

"Where the hell are you? Where you been, Limbo?" I said.

"After all that talk, did you think I was dead, Powell?" He laughingly inquired.

Corbett A. Davis Jr.

"I'm fine, Powell. I'm on my third pitcher of beer sitting here all alone at the Caribbean Club on Key Largo."

"What you doing in Largo?" I asked.

"Had a little business to attend to, but I'll be back tomorrow. We'll get away for a few days and do some fishing. I'll give you a call soon Powell," he quipped as he hung up the phone.

I immediately redialed a stored number.

"Hey, Tracy, it's Powell. How about dinner at my place tonight? Great, I'll pick you up about six. Pack your nightie."

Epilogue

It was the second week of September when Captain Limbo asked me to meet up with him in Boca Grande to fish the beach for "snuke."

"Is that anything like a snook?" I asked laughingly.

He just smiled and shook his head.

Limbo was only the second person I ever knew that referred to the linesiders as "snuke." Gil Drake, an excellent guide whom I met and fished with in Key West, used this term also. When Gil was not chasing bonefish, permit and tarpon in the Keys, he often fished Chokoloskee in the Everglades for redfish, tarpon, and "snuke."

It was ironic that Limbo wanted to fish Boca Grande. I imagine he had forgotten that is where Dawn and I first met. Now it seems like it was so long ago. So much has happened since that day. It would be hard for me to go back and would only stir up some emotions and painful memories.

Reluctantly, I decided to take chance and join my friend.

"Sure Limbo, I'd love to fish Boca Grande with you."

Limbo had not fished that area before. This would be only my third trip.

Gasparilla Island and its port of Boca Grande are famous for many things. Known as the "Tarpon Capital of the World," Boca Grande has been the destination of sports fishermen and their families since the early 1900s. Boca Grande Pass is one of the deepest natural inlets in Florida.

On any given day during the month of June, the pass is cluttered with an assortment of boats. Although no one understands why, thousands of tarpon congregate in the pass in June. An unusual assortment of boats follows closely behind the frothing waters.

That, of course, is not why I agreed to meet Limbo in Boca Grande. By the end of July, the crowds had dwindled. The wealthy northerners and anglers who have come from all over the world have returned home. The tarpon fishing had slowed, the island was empty, and the motels have lowered their rates. Off-season is a beautiful time in any island community, especially on Gasparilla Island and in the town of Boca Grande. When I arrived at the Inlet Lodge, Limbo had already checked in. The attractive older lady behind the counter directed me to a room adjoining Limbo's.

Just as I had feared, memories of Dawn surfaced quickly, memories of a happy meeting so many years ago. I forced myself to stay in exactly the same room as we had then, anxiously waiting for Limbo. I wondered just what was on his mind. I doubted seriously if it had anything to do with snook fishing. He and I still had unfinished conversations that hung like cigar smoke under a ceiling fan.

There was no answer when I knocked on Limbo's door. I figured he probably had taken his binoculars to the beach. Besides tarpon, Boca Grande is home for many great birds. Limbo was probably watching some of the wood storks or ibis. It was here that I first heard white ibis referred to as Chokoloskee chickens. It seems that some of the early settlers who came to the island to fish also enjoyed a good fresh ibis cooked over a hot fire.

I unpacked my clothes and tackle and put them away in the more-than-adequate efficiency. The refrigerator might come in handy, but I wouldn't need the stove. Snook season is closed in September. Even if I wanted to keep one to fry up, I couldn't on this trip.

I backed my sixteen-foot Maverick skiff down the motel's boat ramp and tied it up in slip B-10. The bow was fifteen feet from the back door of my room. I loved this place. Besides having all of the comforts of home, for a moment, it brought back many good memories, though I was sad that Dawn was not here to reminisce about the happy times.

I parked my truck out front, grabbed a cold Corona, and sat on the back porch to wait for Limbo. To the left of the motel was a giant mango tree that was loaded with overly ripe fruit. I walked over, picked up a half dozen or so from the ground beneath the tree, and returned to my chair. As I was peeling the softened mango, a pelican, waiting for a handout, landed on my skiff. I tossed him a piece of the peeling. He tapped it a few times with the tip of his beak before spitting it into the water. He got pissed off and flew away. The antics of the awkward bird helped me to forget my troubles, momentarily causing the grin on my face. I looked on the bow of the Maverick and then at the fleeing pelican. He seemed to have a bigger grin than I did. The damn bird had shit all over my boat. I hosed it off, grabbed another brew, and returned to my chair. Gazing at slip B-10, I remembered the day I got my boat. It was a graduation gift from Mom and Dad. Charles P. Taylor Sr. and Imogene were as proud of their gift as I was. I learned much more from them than I did from all of the twelve years of Catholic education and the four years at Florida State combined. Dad had taught me the jewelry business, responsibility, how to make a living, and, most importantly, how to fish. Mom had taught me how to enjoy all of the above.

I was finishing off my third Corona when I heard Limbo yell out.

"Hey, Powell, how long you been here?"

"Couple hours," I answered.

Limbo had been exactly where I figured. He said he was watching ospreys picking mullet out of the surf.

"Where we gonna eat, Powell?" Limbo asked.

"It's a surprise, Limbo. Get ready, and we'll head that way," I said.

Fishing Boca Grande was a real joy for me. Unlike most of the other places I have fished with Limbo, I actually knew this area better than him. In Boca Grande, I was the captain, and he was the crew. I, for once, could show him how to fish. When I go fishing, it's not just the fishing I enjoy. I like the local food. I like to explore new areas and meet new people. It's the adventure, the bonding, and the stories that make the fishing trips exciting for me. After driving over to Barnacle Bills in Englewood for dinner and the best grouper po'boy in Florida, we returned to the motel. Limbo and I tied up some green and white clousers on a number 2 hook and rigged our tackle. As I was explaining to Limbo how I accidently discovered that snook love green and white clausers, he was giving me a lesson on "snuke."

A few years ago when I had first spotted some snook swimming along the shore of Boca Grande, I asked a guide what fly to use. He told me that in summer months the snook are plentiful but will not eat a fly. I threw about twenty different patterns of deceivers and shrimp imitations at them before deciding that he may be right. Knowing I was wasting my time, I tied on my last choice, a green and white clauser. As soon as the snook saw it, he jumped on it. I caught about eight fish on the same fly. I was a believer.

That was the same day I drove into the local island bank to cash a check. The beautiful blonde teller had suggested my motel and Barnacle Bills Restaurant. A wave of sadness hit me again as I realized Dawn would never be able to visit here again. A feeling of guilt added to my sadness. If it were to get serious between us, I would never allow bad things to happen between Tracy and me. I would never again close my eyes at night without talking to her and appreciating her and all I that have.

With a heart still heavy with guilt, feelings of lost love and the image of Dawn's cold corpse still fresh in my mind, a healthy relationship with Tracy or anyone else seemed unlikely. I only hoped that the pain and sadness would fade with time. My mind suddenly drifted off into an involuntary trance, a hypnotic state near unconsciousness. During those few moments, I felt dazed and in a state of panic that was unexplainable. My conscience was so fragile I imagined Dawn's death as my fault. When I snapped out of my temporary catatonic coma, a state of mind that was happening too often now, Limbo was in the middle of a sentence. He obviously believed I was listening and hearing what he had to say.

By the end of the evening, I knew way more than I cared to about snukes.

Limbo loved the chance to retrieve and share interesting facts from his computer bank of a mind. That was okay with me. I learned more on these fishing trips than you could imagine, and this trip would be no exception.

Some of the things that I found most interesting were not associated with scientific data. I couldn't care less how many spines were found in their dorsal fins or if the posterior nostril was above the level of the upper lip.

I was more concerned with what was going on in Limbo's head. Was he truly dying? Was there really someone out there that he hated enough to kill? Why were we here fishing? What would he confess to next? This new Limbo was more than a concern to me. I worried about his sudden transformation over the recent months. Not only was he drinking again, he also had developed some kind of bizarre spirituality that made him lightheartedly talk about starting his new church, "The Church of Just In Case." I felt as if the only parishioners that he would attract would be prisoners or those facing death. It frightened me to think of Limbo suddenly finding religion.

Limbo must have noticed my lack of interest as I was trying my best to stifle a yawn.

"You look tired, Powell. Let's turn in and get an early start tomorrow," Limbo said.

We agreed to meet in the lobby at six thirty for coffee. My full belly and my Corona buzz allowed for a great long nap.

As we eased away from the dock and idled through the no-wake zone, we passed a couple of old-timers returning from a night of tarpon fishing in the pass. Obviously full of rum and expressing a dislike for flats boats, they were not complimentary as we slid past.

"Fuck me," Limbo said. "Let's go catch snuke."

Obviously, Limbo was not worried with my earlier concerns of his constantly dropping the F-bomb. I couldn't help but smile. It felt good for a moment.

Once I was able to speed up, we were only minutes from the gulf. I ran close to the shore and made sure I went far enough to clear the shallow shoal on the south side.

Limbo pointed to a small pod of tarpon in the middle of about ten boats as I headed the skiff south. If my memory served me, I could find the exact rock pile on shore that produced so many snook on my previous trip. I had the rare chance to show off a little to Limbo. I could impress him with my great fishing knowledge and skills.

After a fifteen-minute run, I beached the skiff in what looked like a deserted area. I explained to Limbo we were on Cayo Costa, an island directly south of Boca Grande Pass. Only accessible by boat, it is a national park and a wildlife refuge.

"It's beautiful here, Powell, but where are the fish?" Limbo said in his best curmudgeonous tone.

"You see those dead mangrove roots down there on the beach," I said as I pointed to an area two hundred yards away. "That's where they live."

We anchored the boat, grabbed our rods, and headed out to waist-high waters. From there, we were only thirty feet from shore and could see any fish that might swim in the natural gut along the shoreline. We were walking parallel to the land on a nice convenient sandbar that also ran parallel to the shoreline. The gut between the beach and us varied in depths from one to six feet. The snook liked these deeper holes because they held bait and provided security.

We waded out another ten feet. With only one back cast, Limbo threw his fly up on the shore and dragged it back into the water. A three-pound snook grabbed the fly only inches from the weathered orange legs of a mature white ibis standing on dry ground. Limbo set the hook gently and his first snuke of the day headed across the bar and out to sea. With Limbo chasing off after him, I hooked one of his buddies. After the normal discussion of "mine's bigger than yours," we took a couple of photos, released them, and continued toward the mangrove roots. I was fishing with a new nine weight STS Scott rod and an Abel reel with floating line that Dawn had given me for Christmas. Limbo, for some unknown reason, was fishing with an antique Pflueger medalist reel and a Lamiglass eight weight rod that looked as if it was built many decades ago. Years earlier, it was the tackle of choice for legendary fly-fishing pioneers such as Lefty Kreh, Flip Pallot, Chico Fernandez, Stu Apte, Jimmie Albright, and Joe Brooks. But now, Limbo looked like an angler from the past with his straw hat, stained T-shirt, and antique tackle. I believe he took pride in his choice of rod and reel.

"It's a challenge. Anybody can catch fucking fish with fancy gear," Limbo muttered when I poked fun at his outfit.

"And another thing," he continued. "You don't have to wear tarpon wear, Columbia, Patagonia, or Marquessas shirts to catch fish. You don't need hundred-dollar wading boots, and you damn sure don't need a hat with a two-foot bill on it. The fish don't give a shit how pretty you are."

"Okay!" I said. "You mean, fish like those right there," I whispered as I pointed to a half-dozen snook.

We caught three or four more fish each before we reached the "snuke hole" of mangrove roots. We stopped, checked our leaders, and tied on fresh flies. I used a pink and white clouser, and Limbo tied on another chartreuse and white one. I could see a black shape under the trees and was quite sure it was a school of snook. There were two snowy egrets wading in the water only inches from the fish. Limbo's cast would have to be very delicate in order not to frighten the birds. To get even with him for making fun of my wardrobe and expensive tackle, I leaned over and quietly whispered, "Limbo, there's about fifteen huge snook under those roots, probably a world record for fly. But you're only going to get one cast at them before you scare those birds and spook the school of fish. So whatever you do, don't fuck it up!"

He didn't see the humor or the fish. His eyes were not quite as sharp as they once were. I told him it was because he didn't have one of those "damned" hats with a two-foot bill. He almost began to smile, caught himself, and resumed his snarl. "What birds?" he asked as a big grin came across his face. When we got within ninety feet of the snook, Limbo started his cast.

Shooting line on two back casts, he laid the fly a foot too long. The leader was across a mangrove root with the fly dangling in the water two inches behind the snook's tail. Limbo made a short three-inch strip. One

Corbett A. Davis Jr.

of the egrets ran down the mangrove root toward the line as a ten-pound snuke turned and swallowed the fly. An explosion of water along with a bloodcurdling screech filled the air.

"What the hell?" Limbo yelled as I was thinking the same thing.

The twelve-pound tippet had wrapped around the leg of the egret the instant the snook ate the fly. The bird was frantically beating the surface of the water with his wings as the snook tried to swim to deeper waters. It was not working. Limbo released tension on the bird by stripping out the line. He hoped it would free the bird, but it did not work. The tired, wet egret jumped into the mangrove roots. Now the line was tangled around the trees, and the bird's head was pulled under the water. Limbo yelled a few instructions, and I took off running. I reached the bird and brought his head up to daylight again. He spit and gasped for a few seconds, and then I believe I heard a sigh of relief as he lay still in my arms. Next, I removed the line from his leg. Something grabbed my eye. The sun was reflecting on the silver belly of the snook floating "fins down." Limbo grabbed his unusual catch and began to revive him by holding him upright, forcing water over his gills.

Unfortunately, it was the biggest snook Limbo had ever hooked, and the bird did all the work. After two or three minutes, we had revived both the egret and the snook. I got a quick photo of Limbo holding up the pair. We then watched as they took off in opposite directions. The egret flew fifty yards down the shore where his mate was pacing in the sand. I was sure there was a curious school of snook waiting close by for the return of their tired old schoolmate.

I was also positive that Limbo, the bird and the "snuke" would tell tales about their adventure for the remainder of their years.

My biggest worry was how much time he had remaining. The thought of losing two close friends was now weighing heavily on my mind. I would soon have my answer, and it was not what I expected to hear.

Limbo asked me to meet him on the back deck that evening for a drink. When I arrived, he had a bottle of thirty-year tawny port, two Cuban cigars, and a strange look in his eyes.

"You okay, Limbo?" I asked as I sat down.

"Sure, Powell," he said as he poured us both a full glass of wine.

"When we talked before, there was one thing I never considered Powell."

For the first time ever, Limbo's color was gone. He had no evidence of spending a lifetime in the sunshine. He was ghostly white.

"What's that?" I said.

"What if I really believed I was going to die and did as I suggested earlier? What if I carried out my revenge in order to enjoy the sweetness of justice done by my own hand? But there was one possibility I did not count on, Powell. What if the chemo and radiation therapy cured my cancer? What if, in fact, I don't die? What would I have to live with then, Powell? And, as my newly formed church asks, what if there is a God? What have I done, my friend?"

My confused mind raced, looking for answers, looking for shelter, a place to hide. I was speechless, and Limbo felt the awkwardness. He sucked down his glass of port, handed me a newspaper, and said, "I'll see you back in Key West."

Limbo disappeared into the darkness.

I put out the cigar, grabbed my glass of port, and found light back in my motel room to read the headlines of the *Miami Herald.*

"Puerto Rican resident and real estate developer, Eve DeMilo, alias Eve Knight, was found murdered in her Key Largo penthouse Tuesday morning. There are no leads and no suspects at this time."